SHOW AND SELL

JUNKYARD DOG COZY MYSTERIES, BOOK 1

SUMMER PRESCOTT

SUMMER PRESCOTT BOOKS PUBLISHING

Copyright 2023 Summer Prescott Books

All Rights Reserved. No part of this publication nor any of the information herein may be quoted from, nor reproduced, in any form, including but not limited to: printing, scanning, photocopying, or any other printed, digital, or audio formats, without prior express written consent of the copyright holder.

**This book is a work of fiction. Any similarities to persons, living or dead, places of business, or situations past or present, is completely unintentional.

CHAPTER ONE

Macy Garson gazed down into the half-empty quart of Rocky Road ice cream and sighed.

"Okay, this is ridiculous. I have to do something," she muttered.

It had been a couple of months since her beloved husband, Jake, had been laid to rest in their Virginia hometown, which seemed very far away from where she now sat in the Florida house that they'd shared for only a short time. Right now, she was wallowing, but she refused to allow herself to stay in the abyss of loneliness and pain for long periods of time, fearing that if she lingered there, she might lose the strength to claw her way back out.

Rising from the couch, Macy went to the kitchen, put the cover back on the ice cream and stashed it in the freezer, where it would be patiently waiting for her next bout of sadness. As soon as she shut the freezer door, she heard the ancient mailbox, which hung tenaciously to the siding just to the right of the front door, squeak open and clink shut.

"Mail. That's something that I can deal with," she murmured, heading to the door.

Macy sifted through the large pile as she headed to the kitchen table to sort it out properly.

"Bill. Bill. Advertisement. Bill," she grumbled, making separate piles of mail for each category.

Facing the growing stack of financial demands struck her with an icy grip that made her shoulders tense and her stomach do a greasy flip-flop.

"What am I going to do?" she whispered, her lower lip trembling.

Jake had a small life insurance policy, but after funeral and travel costs, plus the hospital bills they'd had after the accident, it wouldn't take long before Macy would be struggling to make the payment on their cozy little cottage. She'd filled out what seemed like a thousand applications when they first moved to the small town of Danley, in northeast Florida, but had no luck finding a job.

Her eyes darted back and forth around the kitchen,

her mind racing. They came to rest on a set of canisters that Jake found at a yard sale when they moved to Florida a few months ago. Macy had disliked the avocado green monstrosities because they looked old and somehow disreputable, but Jake had said that they could be just a temporary measure. She'd needed something for her flour, sugar, coffee, and tea, so she'd reluctantly agreed, and had given them a good scrubbing when they brought them home. It hadn't helped their appearance. Nothing could erase that bilious color.

"I could sell those, I bet," she mused. "I wonder how much they might be worth."

Taking her phone out of the back pocket of her jeans, she flipped over to her object identification app and snapped a photo of the canisters. Her mouth dropped open in astonishment.

"Are you kidding me?" she gasped, seeing the online prices for similar canisters.

As it turned out, they were a mid-century modern set that were worth a pretty penny.

"Well, that one is a no brainer. I wonder what else we have that I can sell."

Macy wandered around the house, looking at some of the tired, careworn items through a new lens. She gathered up an assortment of things after researching them on her app and set them on the kitchen table.

"That's a mortgage payment," she murmured, surveying her haul. "Now, how on earth am I going to sell them all?"

She went online and looked to see where similar things were being sold and found a fun site that specialized in vintage and handmade items.

"VendMore," she read the name aloud. "Ready or not, here I come."

Fortunately, there were tutorials to guide her through how to list her items, and before she knew it, Macy had officially opened her online store.

"And now, we wait."

She'd found, during the empty weeks that dragged on after Jake's passing, that keeping busy helped fend off loneliness and self-pity, and at the moment that meant tackling a deep cleaning of the hall bathroom.

"In case I ever have company, I need to make the bathroom sparkle," she reasoned, heading down the hall with a bucket of cleaning products and brushes. Macy winced as she realized she'd been talking to herself again. That had happened quite a bit lately.

The reality that faced her in the bathroom made her sigh. The caulking around the tub needed to be redone, there were cracks in the grout of the tiles in the shower, and it had been a long time since the fixtures had gleamed.

"I can't believe I've lived here for more than three months and never noticed this."

Macy shook her head, hands on ample hips, staring at her challenges.

"Welp, it's not going to clean itself," she muttered, snapping on a pair of nitrile gloves.

She turned on Jake's old clock radio to kill the everlasting silence in the house and got to work, relishing the clean scent of her natural cleansers, and losing herself in scrubbing and polishing and tidying. Macy was on her knees, her jeans practically cutting off the circulation in some places as they bound and creased, when she finally realized that her phone seemed to be blowing up with notifications in her back pocket.

"That's my cue to quit, I guess."

Using the doorframe to brace herself, Macy rose to her feet, her knees popping in protest.

Peeling off the gloves and tossing them on the edge of her now-empty mop bucket, Macy reached for her phone and saw several messages from VendMore.

"Whoa! Four sales already?" Her heart leaped. "Oh geez, I need to find some boxes out in the garage."

Thankful that they hadn't yet disposed of all their moving boxes, Macy searched through the pile, looking for just the right box for each item.

"I'm going to need shipping supplies if this keeps up," she murmured, tilting her head to peek around the stack of boxes that she carried into the house.

Macy boxed up all the items that had sold and had just plopped down, exhausted, into a kitchen chair, when her notification tone went off again. She pulled out her phone and was delighted to see that she had another sale.

"At this rate, I'll have next month's house payment by the end of the week." She blew out a relieved sigh. "Maybe I'm on to something here."

CHAPTER TWO

"Wow, this is the third time you've been in this week," Irma, Macy's favorite postal worker, observed.

The woman looked like she'd been out in the sun for so long that her skin had just turned to leather, and she wore bright blue eyeshadow, no doubt to compliment her bottle blonde hair.

"I know! I'm so excited," Macy confided. "I started this little online business, and it's really taking off."

"Well, good for you, honey," Irma rasped. "Best of luck to ya!"

"Thanks, Irma." Macy beamed and waved on her way out.

The Florida spring sun was relentless, so Macy decided to take a bit of a detour on the way home—one that led her to the Smoothie Shack. She left the drive-thru happily sipping on a Banana Loco and spotted a hand-lettered sign near the entrance of an upscale neighborhood.

"Oooo! A garage sale!" she exclaimed with delight. "I can find things for the house and maybe even find some things to sell."

Macy turned into the manicured neighborhood and kept an eye out for more signs. After a series of twists and turns, she was led by prominent directional arrows to a large ranch house with a driveway and garage jam packed with clean, interesting items.

"Jackpot," she whispered, cutting the engine and practically leaping from the car.

Leaving her smoothie behind, Macy grabbed a handful of reusable shopping bags from the trunk and hurried over to the sale.

"Morning!" a silver-haired couple greeted her.

"How are y'all?" Macy asked, already scoping out some treasures.

"If I were any better, there'd have to be two of me," the woman chuckled.

"That's good to hear," Macy replied with a grin.

"You need any help with anything, just let us know, honey," the woman directed.

"Will do—thank you ma'am."

Macy spotted the leg of a doll sticking up out of a box that had been placed under a card table that was piled high with sweaters. She pulled out the box and had to hold back a gasp. When she'd been researching which things to buy for resale, she'd memorized many of the toys that had been mentioned because she thought it would be fun to sell toys in her shop. Now, right there in front of her, was a Pamela Prettypout doll, in all its glory.

Macy carefully pulled the doll out of the box and examined it. It was flawless. It had been manufactured in the seventies, but it looked as though it had just been taken out of the box yesterday. She eased the doll carefully into one of her totes and continued to dig through the box of toys.

Holy cow!! It's a Melvin the Moving Bear! her brain screamed, when she pulled out a gorgeous long-haired teddy bear and checked his tag. Into the bag he went.

Macy went on to find several vintage toys—three bags full to be exact, and then headed for the jewelry bins that were lined up on a long table, mercifully in the shade of the garage. Her mother, back in the day, had been a bit of a fashionista, so Macy knew quite a bit about vintage jewelry, and this sale had a treasure trove of designer pieces.

A piece of legal-sized yellow paper taped to the front of the table announced that all jewelry pieces were a dollar, unless otherwise marked. Her heart racing like a Daytona speedster, Macy stacked all of the bins and took them over to the couple at the table.

"Can I leave these here while I look for a bit?" she asked.

"Of course you can, sweetie, and if you're buying all that stuff, we'll give you a good deal on it," the woman promised.

"Oh, that's so nice of you, thank you," Macy replied, setting down the bins and the bags of toys that she had filled.

"You're gonna look like Santa Claus going home with all those toys," the husband teased. "Got lots of kids?"

"I'm the biggest kid of them all." Macy laughed softly, managing to dodge the question without bursting into tears. She and Jake had wanted a family.

She hurried through the rest of the tables, picking up four more bags of treasures, very conscious of the fact that she had a banana smoothie melting in her car.

"Okay, I think this'll do it." Macy let out a breath, plopping the last bags on the table in front of the kindly couple. "Let's make a deal." She smiled brightly, hoping that her haul wouldn't break the bank. She'd sold several items already, but the money wouldn't be in her account until next week.

The husband excused himself and went into the house, saying something about a game that was starting, and the wife eyed Macy kindly.

"How 'bout twenty dollars, honey?" she said quietly, glancing about as if to make certain that no one had overheard.

Macy blinked.

"Really? I mean, just one of those bags of jewelry should cost at least…" she began.

The woman laughed and waved off her objections.

"It's just a bunch of old junk cluttering up my house if you ask me. Now are you gonna pay me or not, young lady?" she teased.

"Yes, ma'am, and then I'm gonna hightail it outta here before you change your mind."

Macy reached into her pocket, pulled out a ten and two fives and handed them over. Before she gathered up her bags, the woman reached under the table and pulled out a decorative tin.

"I made some cookies this morning, would you like one?" she asked, opening the tin.

The smell of chocolate chip cookies wafted up and Macy breathed it in with the appreciation that only a true chocolate chip cookie lover can have.

"Yes, ma'am! Can I just tell you how glad I am that I stopped at your sale today?" Macy grinned and took a bite, the explosion of flavor nearly making her eyes roll back in her head. "Oh, this is perfection." She groaned with delight.

"Well, that's kind of you to say. It's my mama's recipe. I'm glad you like it."

"Like doesn't even begin to explain my relationship with this cookie."

Macy finished it in three bites and gathered her bags, thanking the woman again. She loaded her haul into the back of her car and realized that she'd have to put the items in the guest room, where she kept her desk and computer, so that she didn't clutter up the rest of the house while she waited for the new inventory to sell.

Her smoothie was completely liquified and tasted sickly sweet after the carefully crafted flavor of the cookie, so she vowed to pour it down the sink when she got home. Life was too short for subpar smoothies.

"I'm going to order Chinese food tonight, and eat it while I list my new items," she decided, pleased with herself. "At this rate, I'm going to have my mortgage paid for half the year in no time."

CHAPTER THREE

It hadn't been a great morning. After staying up waaaay past her normal bedtime listing the items that she'd bought at the garage sale, Macy had been jolted rudely awake just after seven by the sound of her neighbor's riding lawn mower. Why he needed a riding lawn mower when the yards in their neighborhood were the size of overgrown postage stamps, she had no idea.

After staring into her coffee cup for a good half hour, sipping occasionally, refilling twice, she sighed. The inevitable awaited her. She too, needed to mow, and the longer she waited, the harder it would get. Her earth-loving hubby had gotten an old-fashioned push mower to do their lawn, which had worked out great when he was the one pushing it.

Macy had loved swinging in the porch swing, watching him sweat, his muscles flexing as he took the yard by storm. She had no muscles to flex and was fairly certain that her sweat would not be in the least bit attractive. But it had to be done, and she couldn't afford to pay someone, so she hauled herself out of the kitchen chair, resigned to her humiliating fate, and headed for the bedroom to put on old icky clothing.

Her jean shorts must've shrunk, she reasoned, when she couldn't get them to button, so she reached for a pair of Jakes old basketball shorts—the kind that had an elastic waist and plenty of thigh room. She held the navy-blue shorts for a moment, hugging them tightly…remembering. Her eyes welled and she shook her head.

"Nope. He'd be embarrassed to see the lawn like this, so I can't sit here and feel sorry for myself," she muttered, slipping into the shorts, which hung well past her chubby knees. Going with the oversized men's clothing theme, she tossed on one of Jake's old grubby t-shirts, rolled up the sleeves, and headed for the garage, slipping her iPod into the pocket of the shorts and sticking earbuds in her ears.

Cranking up her favorite '90's tunes, Macy

ventured out of the garage, squinting up at the sky, despite the heavy tint in her sunglasses.

"Really? It couldn't be cloudy today? It had to be hot and humid at eight o'clock in the morning?" she groused, pushing the mower with great effort.

It was awkward, and kind of heavy, but she eventually maneuvered it over to the grass, where the real fun began. With a savage grunt, she pushed it forward, hoping that once her momentum got going it'd be easier. Little did she know there was a faint slope to the yard, so the joy that she experienced pushing the mower quickly toward the curb turned to dismay when she couldn't get it to budge going the other direction.

Frustrated, she leaned on the mower, staring down at it and imagining how fun it would be to take a blow torch to it and turn it into a sculpture.

"I'm smarter than you," she whispered to the beast.

She crossed the lawn with it and pushed it up the driveway, then put it back into position to run it down the hill next to the first stripe that she'd made. She lost track of how many times she had to do that in order to get the front yard done, but it felt like about a million. When she stood at the end of the driveway after the last stripe however, she smiled wanly.

"Showed you who's boss," she told the mower triumphantly.

"Now there's only the backyard left," a voice behind Macy made her jump.

"Oh geez," she exclaimed, pulling the earbuds from her ears. "Sorry, I didn't know anyone was nearby while I was having a conversation with my mower." She smiled wryly.

"No worries. I promise mine an oil change if she behaves." The guy chuckled and Macy couldn't help but wonder who he was and why he was standing in her driveway at this ridiculous hour.

"Ha! Whatever works, I guess," she snickered. "And you are…?"

"Oh, my bad, I thought you might recognize me or something. Umm…I'm Kyle, your neighbor." He turned and pointed to his house. Riding lawn mower guy. She should have known. He was about her age, maybe older, and perfectly ordinary in every way possible. "I can do the back for you if you'd like some help," he offered.

"Oh, thanks, but I've got this," Macy assured him. She was alone in the world now, she might as well get used to doing whatever needed to be done, torturous though it may be.

"Are you sure? It wouldn't be any problem at all."

"Nah, I'm good. Thanks for the offer though." Macy smiled, dying a little inside when she thought of the backyard awaiting her.

"No worries. I'm right next door if you need anything. Hey, I didn't catch your name."

"I didn't throw it," Macy shot back, still smiling. She realized that she was taking out her anger at the world and her circumstances on this poor guy, who was just trying to be nice, and softened. "It's Macy. My name is Macy. Nice to meet you, Kyle," she stuck out a hand with bits of grass on it, then wiped it on her shorts before offering it again.

"Nice to meet you, Macy." He shook her hand and held on just a tad bit too long for comfort, so Macy withdrew and resisted the impulse to wipe her hand on her shorts again.

"Gotta get going," she blurted, practically dragging the mower up the driveway behind her.

"See ya around," Kyle called out.

Macy waved without turning around. She hauled the mower back into the garage and shut the door. The sun had gotten hotter by the second while she mowed the front and there was no way in the world that she was going to do the back right now.

"I had no idea how much Jake did for me," she

whispered, trudging into the house, her once-yellow crocs now a putrid shade of green.

Her eyes welled, and she swallowed past the lump that formed in her throat. Kicking off her ruined shoes, she let the tears roll down her cheeks and headed to the shower. When she caught sight of her pitiful form in the mirror—tearstained cheeks and grass-covered clothing—she shook her head.

"You've gotta do better than this Mace," she told her reflection.

It took several scrubs with her loofa and lemon scented body wash to clean off the green color and bits of dirt that stuck to her feet after slipping into the holes of her shoes, but afterward, Macy felt much better. Stronger somehow. Having to be self-sufficient wasn't a death sentence. Some things wouldn't be as easy for her as they were for Jake, and they might take a bit longer, but she was strong and capable. At least that's what she vowed to tell herself until the day that it was actually true.

After a lunch of leftover Chinese food, Macy headed to Happy Paws. She had signed up to volunteer at the shelter the first week that she and Jake had moved to Danley. When Jake had to take evening shifts at the fire department, she'd happily gone to hang out with dogs and the people who love them.

It was an eclectic bunch of volunteers who ran Happy Paws, and three of them were at the front desk when Macy came in. Polly, a heavyset, middle-aged motorcycle enthusiast with spiky pink hair and enough piercings to set off security devices, was manning the phones, kicked back in an ancient chair with her heavily booted feet on the desk.

Essence, the resident hacker, who perpetually wore flannel, even during the summer, was tapping away at the keyboard of a sad donated computer that she'd turbocharged with some sort of wizardry that the rest of them couldn't even begin to fathom. Her inch-long, glittering purple nails clicked on the keyboard as she worked, and when Macy came in, she lifted her chin in greeting before refocusing on the computer screen.

The last member of the motley crew that was present was Buzz, a grizzled man who loved dogs more than people. No one was sure how old he was, but they'd speculated that he'd probably known George Washington back in the day. Had probably cussed at him, too. Buzz cleaned all of the enclosures several times a day. "Dogs shouldn't live in filth," was his motto, and he muttered it to himself sometimes as he scooped and mopped and rinsed.

"Hey girlie," Polly greeted Macy.

"Hey yourself." Macy grinned.

A cacophony of barking started when the dogs heard her voice. She was there often enough that they knew she was the one who would take them for a walk, if it was their turn.

"Hey guys!" she called out to the dogs, then turned her attention back to Polly. "Who do you have for me tonight?"

"Oh man, we've got a doozy. We walked all the others, but this one just came in maybe an hour ago. They found him tied to a tree behind a house. The owners moved out four days ago," Polly replied, her voice grim.

She cracked her knuckles, obviously thinking about what she'd like to do to the negligent owners. Macy could relate.

"Poor baby. How is he?" she asked.

"Vet said he's healthy—needs some nutrition and love, but…"

"But what?" Macy frowned.

Essence turned and gave Polly a look.

"Well," Polly hedged. "Maybe I should just show you."

"Mmhmm…" Essence pursed her lips, returning to her task.

"Okaaaaaay…" Macy replied, puzzled.

"Come on back." Polly stood and inclined her head toward the door that led to the enclosures.

"Special place in Hades for them people. Don't deserve a dang dog," Buzz muttered, snapping on a pair of rubber gloves and heading for the janitor's closet.

Macy heard a bark that she didn't recognize when they stepped into the hall between the enclosures. Deep, resonant.

"Here we go," Polly said, stopping in front of one of the chain link doors.

"Holy cow!" Macy gasped, taking in the sight of the dog.

"Yep, he's a big baby for sure." Polly nodded.

A master of understatement.

The tawny-colored Great Dane's massive head came nearly up to Macy's shoulder. A thick string of drool dangled from his jowls, and when Macy put her hand up to the fencing, he shook his head, splattering her and Polly.

Macy burst into laughter and wiped her face with the back of her hand. Polly was less amused.

"We tried to get a collar and leash on him, but he wouldn't have it, so we thought you could try to work your magic on him," she said. "Wanna give it a go?"

"Absolutely." Macy's response was automatic.

"You know he's bigger than you, right?" Polly asked.

"He may be taller, but I'm pretty sure I can give him a run for his money weight-wise." Macy chuckled.

"Okay. If you need us, just holler. We'll be watching on the monitors," Polly replied, knowing that Macy liked to work with each animal alone, at least until they were comfortable with her.

"Can I come in?" she asked the majestic canine, noting that he was a bit thin and that his eyes held a heart-wrenching sadness.

He snorted and shook his head again, which Macy took as a good sign. She slowly lifted the latch on the gate and slipped inside, closing it behind her. The dog backed up a step, watching.

Macy's heart beat fast.

"We don't even know your name, sweet boy," she murmured, looking into a pair of wary blue eyes. "You're beautiful, aren't you?"

She made a fist and offered the back of her hand to him for a sniff. He lowered his head and sniffed intently.

"That's it. See who I am," Macy cooed.

The dog slurped his tongue across the back of her hand, then reared up and planted his front paws on her shoulders, nearly knocking her over as he towered above, the string of drool precariously close to her chin.

"Okay, good boy. We're friends now," Macy gasped, using every bit of her strength to keep her feet planted so that she wouldn't fall. "Do you know commands? Can you sit?"

He sat.

"Oh, good boy!" Macy exclaimed, reaching out a hand to gently stroke the side of his face. He whimpered and leaned into her hand. Tears sprang to her eyes, but she pulled herself together immediately. She had to be strong to support the dog. Emotions could come later.

"Let's give you a name. I'm going to call you Leo, because you're like a majestic lion. Does that work for you, huh, Leo?"

He cocked his head and lifted a paw, reaching out toward her.

"Oh, you know how to shake, Leo? Good boy," she encouraged, taking his paw and shaking it. "Good boy, Leo."

Macy released his paw and rubbed between his ears.

"Do you like to go for walks, Leo?" she asked. The dog sprang into action, taking joyous laps around the enclosure and finally leapt up to put his paws on her shoulders again, this time bathing her face in a sloppy kiss.

"Oh yuck." She giggled. "I'm going to take that as a yes. Okay, good boy. Down, Leo."

She snapped her fingers, and Leo sat.

"Good boy. Now, let's get this leash on you."

She didn't bother with a collar, because when she reached for it, his eyes went so wide that the whites showed, and he recoiled.

"I see," Macy said softly. "Don't worry, you're safe, Leo."

She reached for the leash and looped the end of it. She showed it to Leo, letting him sniff it, then slipped it gently over his head. He stood and wagged his tail.

Macy reached for the latch to the enclosure, and Polly opened the door at the end of the hall.

"Hey, Mace… I don't want to be a Debbie Downer here, but … do you really think you can handle him with just a leash looped over his head?" she asked, her eyes on Leo.

"He'll be fine," Macy assured her.

"You sure?"

"Positive."

Polly sighed, skeptical. "Okay. I'll get the team ready just in case."

The shelter team watched her walk him out of the building and around the small pond behind it, mouths agape. Leo was magnificent. He gained confidence with each step and strode perfectly beside Macy as though they'd been friends forever. When she took him back inside, she gave him a treat and a big kiss on the top of his sleek head and said goodnight.

"Girl, you got some kind of voodoo going on with those dogs," Essence observed, when Macy came back into the office. "That thing looks like he could eat me for lunch."

"Nah, you'd be an afternoon snack at most," Macy teased.

"You coming to game night at my place tonight, Voodoo Queen?" Polly asked.

"Wouldn't miss it." Macy grinned.

CHAPTER FOUR

Feeling refreshed after a long shower to scrub away the last vestiges of Great Dane drool, Macy flopped down onto the couch to munch on a healthy salad that she pretended to enjoy as much as the pizza that stared up at her from the pages of her coupon book.

She channel surfed for a while before catching sight of a home that she recognized on the noon news.

"Hey, that place looks familiar," she murmured, putting down her fork and turning up the volume.

She read the headline scrolling across the bottom of the screen, while a solemn reporter yammered on about something. *Local Woman Murdered.*

Then it hit her. She DID recognize that house.

When they flashed a photo of the victim on the

screen, Macy gasped. It was the kindly older woman who had given her the world's best chocolate chip cookie, along with a steal of a deal, at her garage sale.

Stunned, Macy slowly finished her salad, then, feeling entirely unsatisfied by her fully adult dinner, she made a beeline to her office to look at the things that she'd bought from a woman who was now a murder victim.

Macy eased down onto the floor and gently unloaded the bags filled with jewelry into a large shallow plastic bin so that she could sort through it. From what she could tell at a glance, it was all costume jewelry, but some of it was mid-century designer costume jewelry that would bring in a pretty penny. She felt the slightest twinge of guilt knowing that she was going to make way more money selling these than she'd shelled out to buy the whole lot of it, but something told her that the woman knew the jewelry was valuable and just wanted to part with it. It sort of made sense. She could've worn a different set of jewelry every day for a few years and still not wear all of it. It would take Macy quite a while to list it all, but she knew it would be worth it.

She went through a packed jewelry box that had come with her haul, plucking out interesting pieces to research, based upon their style, designer stamp and content stamp. There were quite a few that contained precious metals and what looked like precious stones. One particular piece caught her eye, and she picked it up carefully, unwinding the delicate gold chain from the twists and strands that tried to hold it captive in the box.

It was a gold locket, with a dainty diamond perimeter, and what looked like a ruby in the center.

"Oh wow," Macy whispered, examining it. It was clearly old, and it was flawless.

She lifted the tiny gold clasp that held the locket closed, then pried the two halves open with her thumbnail. Inside, she discovered a black and white photo of a young couple on their wedding day, and Macy very carefully wiggled it out, trying mightily not to damage the photo. She turned it over once she'd freed it, and on the back was a series of numbers, separated by dashes.

"Interesting. I wonder if that's an old phone number or something," she murmured. "There are too many numbers for it to be a date."

The realization that she was holding onto and pawing through the property of a murder victim struck hard, making Macy shiver. She placed the photo and locket back into the jewelry box and feeling silly and superstitious, went to the closet, pulled up a loose floorboard that she had found when they first moved in, and tucked the box down into the space below.

"I wonder why she was murdered." Macy mused, chewing on her lower lip after replacing the floorboard. She felt quite certain that there was a story behind the sweet old lady getting murdered, and she couldn't shake the thought of it.

"Super sad, but not my problem, I guess." She sighed and rolled over onto her knees so that she could get up more easily. "I've gotta get in shape," she muttered, as her knees creaked in protest. "Just walking the dogs isn't going to cut it."

When she went to her refrigerator to scope out the possibilities, Macy was frustrated that it was devoid of anything with which to make a decent snack. She missed standing beside her gorgeous hunk of a man while he chopped and diced all sorts of flavor-filled healthy things for their meals and snacks.

With a sigh of deep resignation, Macy accepted the fact that she was just going to have to do one of the things that she loathed. It was time ... to go to the grocery store. The cruel place that was filled with all the things that she *wanted* to eat, sitting right next to the things that she *should* eat. She'd stepped inside the air-conditioned maw at the entrance so many times, fully intending to purchase wholesome fresh food and ending up coming out with things that were sweet, salty, crunchy, and filled with chemicals that she couldn't even pronounce. And don't even get her started on calories.

Macy pushed her cart down the aisles, passing cookies, chips, and the entire bakery section with grim determination. She was going to battle with food, and she would win. So intent was she upon her quest for healthy food that she nearly jumped out of her skin when a kindly older man spoke to her from behind while she was carefully examining a display of bell peppers.

"You look familiar, young lady," he commented.

Macy whirled to face him, pepper in hand. Her ample rump bumped the lowest row of peppers and to her horror, they started sliding. She put her hands out in a vain attempt to catch them, but there were still several that landed on the polished linoleum with polite little thuds.

"Oh no," she uttered, feeling her face turn beet red.

"Accidents happen," the older man said, bending to help.

Side by side, they gathered up the wayward peppers. A grocery store employee hurried over.

"I'm so sorry," Macy blurted, quite sure that her face was the same color as the employee's crimson vest.

"No worries, ma'am," the early twentysomething young man told her. "I'll take it from here," he said, quickly gathering up all of the remaining peppers on the floor.

"I can like, pay for those or whatever," Macy offered, a desperate plea that was more about forgiveness than value.

"Nah. Happens all the time. They're probably not even bruised," the young man assured her.

"Oh, okay." Macy was still embarrassed but figured that her best course of action was to walk away. She plunked the last pepper in her hand onto the now askew pile, and it slid again, dumping nearly all of the peppers in the display onto the floor.

"You've got to be kidding me!" she bleated, beginning to bend down to pick them up.

The young man stopped her with upheld hands.

"I'll just take it from here," he insisted with an unshakeable smile. "Just … enjoy the rest of your shopping."

Macy took hold of her cart and steered it around the mess, muttering a thank you on her way by. She caught sight of the older man who had helped her, standing by the tomatoes, a bemused expression on his face.

"Thanks for helping me out. I'm such a klutz sometimes." Macy shook her head, then looked at the man more closely. "Do I know you from somewhere?"

"Maybe you've seen me around the neighborhood," he shrugged. "Although you look familiar too, like I said earlier."

"Before the pepper avalanche." Macy smiled wanly.

"Indeed. I just came in to see if this store might allow me to put up flyers for my yard sale, and thought I'd pick up some things for my dinner while I was at it."

"Oh! You're having a yard sale? I love yard sales," Macy brightened, forgetting all about the pepper mishap, though she'd internally vowed to never eat peppers again, if she could help it.

"Well then, you ought to come by. If you have a piece of paper, I'll give you the address. It's my mom's place, and she has a ton of stuff. Lots of jewelry, clothes, knick-knacks. It all has to go. I'll be selling things cheap, just to get rid of them. She's moving into a retirement home."

"Oh, okay." Macy nodded. "I don't have a piece of paper, but I can put the address in my phone," she added, taking the phone out of her oversized pink leather purse.

"Awesome, thanks," she said when he gave her the address.

"Hope to see you there." The man smiled. "Are you a collector, or do you just love yard sales?"

"Actually, I started a new business recently where I find things at garage sales and sell them in an online shop," Macy admitted.

"Well, isn't that fun? What's the name of your shop?" he asked.

"The Junkyard Dog. I volunteer for the animal shelter and donate to them every month, so I thought that would be a cute name for my shop."

"You're a busy young lady." The man gave her an approving smile.

"Yep, I guess I am." Macy's expression was wistful. She knew how to fill her days, mostly, but no one realized how much time she spent staring at the ceiling when sleep eluded her. She shook off the moment. "But, I'm a busy lady who needs to buy her dinner and get back home. Thanks again for helping me with the peppers."

"You're more than welcome. Hope to see you on Saturday." He raised a hand in farewell and headed toward the bakery department.

"See you then."

Macy shot a glance over at the clerk who was still picking up peppers, then hurried away, grabbing a box of mushrooms on her way to the meat counter. Rushing through the store as though she was being timed, Macy completed her shopping and headed home. After she put her groceries away and turned on the television, she was immediately greeted with another station covering the story of the murdered woman. There were no suspects, and apparently not even any leads, according to the anchor.

Macy shivered, thinking of the dead woman's jewelry in her closet. Heaving herself up out of the comfort of her overstuffed couch, she headed for the office. She would clean all of the late woman's jewelry in her ionizer and list it so that she could get it out of the house as soon as possible. Same thing for all the toys that she'd bought. Even though she knew she was being ridiculous and superstitious, she didn't want the former belongings of a murder victim in her house. That couldn't possibly contribute to creating a Zen environment.

Inspired, she cleaned all of the items and listed each and every one of them. When she looked at the clock, she groaned. "Oh man, I have like two minutes to get ready for game night at Polly's," Macy lamented. "Guess they'll just have to see me in all my messy glory."

CHAPTER FIVE

Macy double-checked the address twice when she pulled up in front of Polly's house. The tidy bright yellow home, trimmed out in crisp white, with immaculate window boxes filled with flowers wasn't quite what she had expected. It was all very cozy-looking and traditional, and Polly...wasn't.

There were a few other cars parked in front of the yellow house though, and when Macy killed the engine, she saw Sync, one of the other dog walkers from the shelter, getting out of an ancient car that was painted with rainbows, flowers, and symbols of various kinds.

"Hey, Sync," she greeted him.

"Namaste," he replied, putting his hands together in front of his heart chakra.

Macy had always admired his long, flowing chestnut hair, and she loved that he could be counted on to be in a good mood, no matter what the turn of events.

"Do you even eat pizza?" she asked, falling in step beside him as they approached the house.

"I'm fasting at the moment, so pizza isn't a part of my universe."

"Okay cool, well I'll celebrate your fasting by eating your share," Macy teased.

"Sometimes we need food for the body, other times, food for the soul."

"I have no idea what that means, but it sounded really profound," Macy replied.

"Profound thoughts are a natural consequence of fasting." Sync grinned.

"Don't you get hungry though?"

"Totally. I'd say I could eat a horse right now, but I have too much respect for our equine friends."

"Good. I'm not the only one who's starving then." Macy giggled, and Sync rang the doorbell.

"Come in, it's open!" they heard Polly holler from inside.

Sync opened the door and stood back to let Macy enter.

"Ladies first? What a gentleman," Macy remarked.

"Nah, I'm just an introvert. I don't like being the first one to enter a room. Throws off my chi." Sync shrugged.

"Well, heck, we wouldn't want to do that." Macy chuckled.

It felt so good to be among friends, just having a good time, sharing some bad-for-you food, and playing wonderfully cutthroat board games with a group of kindhearted misfits who didn't actually care who won. It had been quite a while since Macy had laughed without feeling guilty. She was still mourning Jake, and whenever her wicked sense of humor got the best of her, she'd felt guilty. Tonight was different. Tonight was a breakthrough that she knew Jake would've wanted for her, and it felt like a giant weight had been lifted from her shoulders.

"So, do you have big plans for this weekend, Miss Thang?" Essence asked Macy, in between giant sips of diet soda that she drank from a rhinestone-studded travel mug. Her lips left a ring of purple lipstick on the bubblegum pink straw.

"Oh, big time," Macy drawled sarcastically. "I'm going to a garage sale. This guy in the grocery store said he was having one and gave me the address."

"Oh yeah?" Polly perked up. "Where is it? I might want to go too. I'm always on the lookout for Nancy Drew books."

The other three turned to stare at her.

"What? I had them as a kid. It's nostalgic." She glared.

"I mean, that's totally cool," Macy swooped in to reassure her. "The address is 11362 Newton Road."

"Wow, I didn't know the numbers went up that high on Newton Road," Polly mused.

"Yeah, that's gotta be way out in the country." Essence nodded. "Good luck with that."

Sync frowned. "You need to be really careful about things that you buy at garage sales," he warned.

"Yeah, bugs and stuff." Essence shuddered.

"No, not bugs. Or not just bugs, anyway," Sync clarified. "You never know what kind of energy might be attached to different objects. You don't know what the people who owned them might've been through."

Essence pursed her lips and stared at him. "There he goes again with that magical mystery stuff. I swear you give me nightmares, Sync."

"Well, she needs to know," Sync replied, gently. "Things at garage sales might have all kinds of negative vibes about them."

"I mean, I've seen some seriously creepy dolls." Polly nodded.

"It's not so much about creepiness of the objects themselves, it's the negative emotions surrounding them," Sync held out his hands as though an object rested in them. "Like, a pretty set of crystal glasses might have belonged to a divorcing couple. There might be an odd number because someone broke one in a fit of anger."

"Or it could've belonged to someone who died," Essence pointed out matter-of-factly.

"Yeah, exactly!" Sync beamed, thrilled to be understood at last.

"That's why I buy everything online, thank you very much," Essence declared, grabbing her purse. "I wouldn't go out in the country looking for a bunch of stuff that belonged to somebody else. Sounds like a horror movie waiting to happen." She waved a hand as if to erase the image from her mind, then stood to go.

"Well, I have a mortgage, so unless I find a better way to pay it, I'm going to as many garage sales as I can find." Macy shrugged.

"At least let me come over and cleanse the residual auras with some crystals," Sync requested, his eyes filled with compassion.

"I'll let you know what I find." Macy bit the inside of her lip so that she wouldn't burst into a fit of the giggles.

Essence headed to the door, muttering something about amateur warlocks, and the rest of the gang trailed after her, Polly bringing up the rear.

"Oh! I forgot to tell you guys," Macy blurted, when they were all standing on Polly's porch, saying their goodbyes. "You know that lady that got murdered the other day? That was like two days after I went to her garage sale and bought a bunch of stuff. She gave me such a great deal. Her chocolate chip cookies were amazing too."

Sync clapped a hand over his mouth and shook his head, eyes closed.

"Girl, you'd better get that stuff out of your house like yesterday!" Essence exclaimed, wide eyed.

"She's so right." Sync nodded vehemently.

"I can't imagine why someone would murder such a sweet lady," Macy mused.

"Because people are evil," Essence proclaimed.

"Fact," Polly agreed.

"Not true, we are beings of light," Sync said quietly.

"I'm about to light my way home. See y'all on Tuesday." Essence waved and headed to her car, and

Sync wandered toward his, hands in his pockets, a wistful look on his face.

"Hey, Mace," Polly whispered, beckoning her closer.

"Yeah?"

"If you go to that garage sale and find a No-No Nancy doll, my sister would really love it. She had one as a kid, and it got lost in a move. She still talks about that silly thing."

Macy grinned. "I think we all want to go back to childhood every now and then. Seeing some of the toys from that time helps us do that. I'll keep my eyes open for a No-No Nancy."

"Thanks kid. See ya soon."

"See ya. And thanks again for game night. I really needed it."

"Same here," Polly said.

For a moment, their eyes met, and Macy saw what might have been a shadow of sorrow that she'd never seen before. Polly nodded quickly and turned away, stepping back inside.

CHAPTER SIX

Macy was tired when she got home from game night, but it was a good kind of tired. The kind of tired that gave her hope that she might get a full night's sleep. Those had been few and far between since the accident.

When she closed the door behind her and flipped on the living room light, Macy gasped, her heart pounding.

"Wha…?"

She couldn't even form a coherent thought as she froze in the living room, staring at items strewn about in the hallway in front of her office. They were garage sale items. Hurrying over to the doorway, Macy was horrified to see that her office/merchandise room had been turned upside down.

"But wait ... the front door was locked," she whispered to herself.

The terrifying thought crossed her mind that the intruder might still be in the house. Macy grabbed a vintage golf club and headed down the hall to her room, fury coexisting with abject fear. She sagged against the wall of her room when she snapped on the overhead light and realized that it was empty. There was no one lurking, even in the closet, which had also been tossed.

"What is going on?" she hissed, club held high and ready to strike.

Her heart threatening to pound out of her chest, Macy stood in front of the closet, thinking.

"The back door..." She realized with dread. "If they didn't come in the front door, they must have come in the back door.

She moved stealthily down the hall and through the kitchen, turning on lights as she went. When she saw what awaited her, just inside the back door, she let out a shriek, dropped the golf club, and leaped up onto the kitchen counter with finesse that she didn't know she had.

Dancing from foot to foot and choking out horribly guttural, nonsensical sounds, she peered down at the floor, feeling faint and nauseated.

"911… I have to call 911." She was practically hyperventilating at this point.

When she pulled her phone out, her shaking fingers fumbled it and nearly sent it tumbling to the floor.

"No!" she screamed, securing it in an iron grip.

She dialed 911 and tried to get her breathing under control well enough to speak at least semicoherently to the dispatcher.

"911, what is your emergency?"

"There … there was a break-in. Someone broke into my house."

Macy's voice shook, and she swallowed hard against the bile that threatened to rise in her throat.

"Where are you now, ma'am? Are you in the house?"

"Yes, I'm in the house, and I'm trapped. Can you please send somebody right away?"

"You're trapped? Is the intruder in the house with you?"

"No. No, the intruder is gone." Macy was trying her best not to cry.

"Are you hurt?"

"No, I'm scared," Macy admitted, aware of the fact that her hands were ice cold, even with the warm humid air flowing into the kitchen through the open back door.

"Because you're trapped?"

"Uh-huh."

"By what?" the dispatcher asked.

"A snake."

Macy trembled from head to toe, as if saying the word had given the beady-eyed, slithering beast superpowers. A thought struck her that made her go deathly still ... could they climb vertical surfaces?

"A snake," the dispatcher repeated, as though she hadn't heard properly.

"Yes, could you please tell them to hurry? My back door is open, but it's not going out."

"So ... was there an intruder other than the snake?" the dispatcher asked.

"Of course there was an intruder. Snakes can't break into houses ... oh geez ... can they? I mean, no, this one obviously didn't, because someone went through all my stuff, but ... like ... snakes can't really shimmy in through closed doors, can they?" Macy's teeth chattered at the thought.

"You're not from here, are you ma'am?" the dispatcher drawled.

"No, I'm definitely not. I'm not from here, and I don't belong here with the snakes and gators and bird-sized mosquitos." Macy's voice cracked on the last word, and she could've sworn that she heard the dispatcher sigh.

"Stay on the line. I'm sending a car out. They should be with you shortly."

"Thank you so much, but can I ask you a question…?"

"Yes ma'am."

"Can snakes climb vertical surfaces?"

"Depends on the surface and the size of the snake. If they're big enough they can climb just about anything."

Macy gagged.

"You okay, ma'am?"

"No, I'm not. Are they close?"

"They're on their way."

"Tell them to come to the back door, but to be careful, because that's where … it … is."

Without the use of lights or sirens, which Macy thought was terribly rude, a squad car arrived, and the dispatcher hung up, seeming to suddenly be in a hurry.

"Officers, be careful!" Macy screamed, pointing at the snake, who slithered under the edge of the kitchen cabinets when the policemen drew near.

One was short and stout, the other was a ginormous mountain of a man. Both had buzz cuts and permanent tans.

"That's your intruder?" the short one asked, not even bothering to hide his amusement.

"No, of course not, that's the snake," Macy practically shouted. "Can you please just…shoot him or something?" she begged.

"No, ma'am, can't shoot anything inside city limits, unless it's an imminent threat," Officer Mountain said, with a grin.

"It doesn't get much more imminent than this. He's right there, like less than four feet from me." Macy pointed, dancing from one foot to another on the worn Formica countertop.

"Aww, he's just a li'l ole gopher snake. He won't hurt ya," Officer Teapot said, reaching down to pick up the horrible squiggling nightmare.

Macy shrieked.

"Get it out, get it out right now." She hopped up and down on the counter, which groaned beneath her.

The short officer left through the back door and came back empty handed.

"What did you do with it?" Macy whispered.

"I let him go. He was harmless."

"Wait." Macy's eyes went so wide that she was

sure the whites were showing all the way around. "Where did you let it go?"

"Took him out there and set him down on the far side of your fence."

"How could you? I'm never going to be able to go outside again," Macy wailed.

Mountain seemed to be growing impatient.

"You'll be fine," he said, sounding bored. "You told the dispatcher that there was an intruder?"

"Yes, that's why the back door is open. I don't leave doors open," Macy replied, still perched on the counter.

The officers examined both sides of the door.

"No sign of forced entry, but this lock is so old that anybody with a credit card could open it," Teapot mused.

"Well, that's just great." Macy sighed and ran a hand through her hair, her heart rate beginning to slow to a more normal pace now that her reptilian adversary was no longer on the kitchen floor. "I guess I'll put a chair under the knob until I can get a locksmith out here," she muttered to herself.

"Ma'am could you come down from there and show us why you think someone broke into your house?"

"Yeah, but…could you please just look around

under the edge of the cabinets to make sure that the snake didn't like ... bring a friend with him or something?" Macy asked.

Mountain gave her a look but bent over and shined his flashlight under the edges of the kitchen cabinets.

"You're clear," he barked. "Now, can you show us the damage?"

Macy took them to her office first.

"It's usually really neat in here." She gestured to the mess all over the floor and the emptied plastic bins.

"That's quite a bit of stuff," Teapot remarked, exchanging a glance with Mountain.

"Yeah, I have a reselling business."

"You got receipts for all this stuff?" Mountain asked.

"Are you kidding me right now? I called you, remember? Because I had an intruder. I don't live like this, with stuff scattered all over the floor. And now you want to ask me about receipts? I don't like your insinuations."

Both officers merely stared at her, arms folded.

"No. I don't have receipts. I got almost all of this stuff at garage sales. Garage sales don't give receipts," Macy finally replied, sullen.

"Can you determine whether or not anything is missing?" Teapot asked.

"In this mess? How? I didn't even touch anything because I thought you guys might need to take fingerprints or something." Macy fumed.

"Got any enemies?" Mountain asked, eyeing her with what looked like suspicion.

"Aside from that dumb snake? No, not that I can think of. I'm new here. My husband passed a few months ago, after we moved in, so I don't really know anybody well enough to make an enemy."

"New in town, huh?" Teapot's eyes narrowed.

"Yeah, and I'm a darn Yankee too. You gonna hold that against me?" Macy snapped.

"Got security cameras?" Mountain asked.

"Sure, yeah, a dozen of them. My back door lock is so ancient that a child could break in, but I've invested in lots of other security. I mean seriously," Macy ranted, frustrated, adrenaline from her slithery encounter still coursing through her.

"I'm pretty sure I could catch that snake and bring him back in if you'd like," Teapot threatened.

Macy froze, glaring at him.

"I think we have enough to go on," Mountain commented, ending the conversation. "We'll be in touch if we find something."

"Which you won't." Macy sighed.

"Most likely not," he agreed. "Small time breaking and entering and they didn't steal anything…" Mountain shrugged, leaving the sentence hanging, unfinished, between them.

"Well, thanks for taking the snake away anyhow," Macy muttered.

"Next time just get a broom and sweep him on out," Teapot suggested, his tone so patronizing she wanted to scream.

"Yeah, that's just what I'll do."

CHAPTER SEVEN

When the officers left, Macy took one of her kitchen chairs and wedged it under the doorknob of the back door, then took the other and wedged it under the front doorknob. Still shaking and weak at the knees, she scanned the floor with every step she took, just in case her reptilian nemesis had brought any friends with him.

The prescription of choice for soothing her jangled nerves was lavender tea and popcorn, with a healthy dose of television. Her normal preference for TV—crime shows—was out. She'd had enough of weird and scary circumstances for one day, so she turned on a popular sitcom that she barely heard, even when she tried hard to lose herself in the madcap show.

Eventually, the lavender tea started to have a calming effect, and Macy rolled her head from side to side to relax, wincing at the crackles and pops. Despite the easing of tension, she still flinched at every creak and groan of her cozy little house. The wind that made her palm tree sway brought with it sounds of the night that unnerved her all over again.

"Why would someone break into this place?" she muttered at the television, while a commercial about breakfast cereal danced across the screen. "I mean, seriously. I have nothing. This is a tiny house in a modest neighborhood. Who scopes it out and says, hey, let's go dig for money in the couch of the poor widow who can't even mow her lawn without figuring out a life hack?"

Disgusted with the fact that she was sitting there feeling sorry for herself, Macy took her half-full bowl of popcorn and set it in the microwave so that it wouldn't get stale—she was never one to waste perfectly good popcorn, although there was almost never popcorn left in the bowl to waste—double-checked the chairs wedged under both doorknobs, turned off the lights, and headed to bed with the rest of her tea.

Macy seriously considered taking an allergy pill to help her sleep, though her allergies were currently stable, but decided against it. If someone wanted to break into her house again, she wanted to be awake enough to deal with it. Just how she'd deal with it, she had no idea, but various scenarios flooded her brain as soon as she pulled up the covers.

She tossed, she turned. She gave up for a while and played a game on her phone. She tossed and turned more, and finally, she dropped off—sheer emotional exhaustion taking its toll. The insistent ringing of her phone woke her from her fitful slumber in the morning, and she practically leaped for it, irrationally hoping that it might be the police, reporting that they'd caught her intruder. Instead, it was the locksmith, who had received her emergency message from the night before. Of course, since she wasn't yet ready to face the day, he informed her that he'd be there in ten minutes or less.

With a groan, Macy threw the covers back and scrambled to find the closest clothing that she could throw onto her body. Settling for a hooded sweatshirt that had seen a few too many washings, and a pair of yoga pants that had never actually been used for yoga, she slipped them on, tossed her hair up into a ponytail and brushed her teeth. She may not look great when the locksmith came, but at least she wouldn't knock him over with morning breath.

Before she could even finish making her coffee, the locksmith showed up. When she let him in, he hitched up his belt and asked her to show him the back door. On her way through the kitchen, she flipped the switch so that her coffeemaker would begin the magical process of creating the beverage that helped her get through the day without—mostly —letting the things that were going on in her head slip out in public.

"Yer husband know how to change out a lock set?" the repairman asked, perusing the flimsy lock that was currently on the door.

"I don't have a husband." Macy sighed, cringing at how awful those words sounded coming from her mouth. The truth of it was that she really didn't want to unload her situation on the locksmith, only to see the pitying looks that inevitably would be cast in her direction.

"Single girl like you oughta be more careful about home security. It's a crazy world out there," he mused.

"And that would be why you're here. Can you fix it?" Macy asked, trying very hard to not let her lack of caffeine override her civility.

"Yep. But if you keep that same lock on the front door, fixing this one ain't going to do you no good."

Macy counted quickly to five before she answered. "Then can you fix both of them while you're here?"

"Yep."

Glad that he was a man of few words, Macy let him know that she'd be in earshot if he needed her and let him go about his business. She went to her office/guest room and started listing items in her store. As much as she loved her budding new business, the stacks of items were starting to get to her. The more she listed, the more she would sell, and the cleaner her office would be.

Macy listened for the coffee pot to signal her that its process was done, with the typical series of gurgles and burbles, and the second that she heard it, she practically sprinted to the kitchen for a cup. The locksmith, fortunately, was absorbed in his task and didn't offer any conversational tidbits.

When at last he'd finished with both doors and presented her with a bill that nearly made her gasp, Macy handed him her credit card and was glad that she'd been able to list so many items while he worked. The unexpected expense had cut into her budget for the month. She tried not to fidget while he entered all of her credit card info into his phone by hand, because his chip reader didn't work. After the transaction, she practically pushed him out the door, grabbed her purse, and headed for the garage sale out in the country that the man in the grocery store had told her about.

"This can't be right." Macy frowned at her phone.

According to her maps app, she was at the exact address that the man had given her. The only problem was that there were no homes, nor garages, or people for that matter, in sight. She was in the middle of nowhere, with only the buzzing of insects and twittering of birds for company.

She sat, perplexed, looking in every direction to see if she had missed something. When she craned her neck to see behind her, she saw a car in the distance that was heading her way. She got out of the car to flag it down, ignoring the errant thought that it might not be her best decision.

An older gentleman pulled over his boat-sized car and rolled the window down.

"Hey there. Ya lost?" he asked, fortunately not looking anything at all like a serial killer.

"I'm not sure. My phone is telling me that the address I'm looking for is right here, but there clearly is nothing here, so I'm wondering if my phone is glitching or something. Would you mind looking up an address for me?"

"You betcha." The man nodded and pulled out his phone, tapping the address in. "Mine says you're here too. That's kinda crazy. Hope you're not missing anything important."

Macy smiled ruefully. "Nah, not really. There was supposed to be a garage sale at this address, that's all."

"Welp, good luck to ya then, young lady." The man raised a hand in farewell, rolled up his window, and went on his way.

"Thanks," Macy replied, distracted. "Well now what?" she muttered to herself, once the car was out of sight.

She leaned against her car and thought for a moment.

"Hi there!" A voice from behind nearly made Macy jump out of her skin, and she whirled toward it.

A young man emerged from the bushes near the side of the road, wearing a backpack, and came striding toward her like it was the most natural thing in the world.

"You lost?" he asked.

"No. Yes. I guess so," Macy sputtered. "I was just ... looking for a garage sale."

"Out here? Good luck with that." The guy chuckled, looking around. "Hey, would you mind giving me a ride?"

"Sorry, I can't. It's ... against company policy," Macy stammered, opening her door and practically leaping back inside the car. She locked the doors, cranked the engine, and left him standing in the dust, staring after her.

CHAPTER EIGHT

Frustrated by her inability to find the particular garage sale that had ended up leading her on a wild goose chase, Macy cruised around some of the nicer areas back in town to hunt for other sales. There were three more that she found, but none yielded anything of interest for her business, so she decided to call it a day and headed for home.

Ensconced in her favorite spot on the couch, bowl of popcorn to her right, glass of diet soda on the end table to her left, Macy grabbed the remote and turned on the television, needing a break after the strange events of the past few days. Her respite was short lived, however. As soon as the TV clicked on, she saw continuing coverage of the murder case.

Fascinated, she turned up the volume and munched on popcorn while she took in the details. The woman was a local librarian. *Well, that explains why she was so nice.* Her name was Lisa Greitz, and she was apparently very active in the local community. There were no clues that had surfaced, at least that they mentioned, and there were no suspects.

"Wow, her poor family must be losing their minds," Macy murmured, knowing all too well what fresh grief felt like. "I've gotta find out more about her. Who knows, maybe there's something that I can do to help."

Setting the popcorn bowl aside, Macy retrieved her laptop from her office, eternally thankful that whoever had broken in hadn't bothered it in the least, and brought it back out to the couch with her, letting the news play in the background while she did some digging.

"Whoa, Lisa came from a wealthy family," she mused, scanning the screen. "Society page photos, charity events, lots of family stuff, but no pics with her husband. I wonder if she married down. That's so sad. He's such a nice guy from what I could tell."

She scrolled further through the entries under Lisa's name and stopped short.

"Hmmm ... what have we here? Lisa is getting a community service award at the country club, and the lady standing next to her doesn't exactly look happy about it."

She had to enlarge the photo to read the names underneath.

"Let's see who you are, Miss Rich Sourpuss... Ah, there it is, Regina Risinger. Makes sense, she even has a mean-girl name," Macy commented. "I'm gonna track you down, girl."

Roughly two hours, a hotdog, and a peanut butter and jelly sandwich later, she'd found a ton of information about Regina Risinger and her relationship to Lisa.

"You two were rivals in everything," Macy commented, chewing on a bite of licorice, her after lunch sweet treat. "Tennis, golf, bridge, and even charity stuff. You might be a good murder suspect, lady. Ah-ha! There it is... I'm going to come see you at work."

Without giving herself time to think about it, other than coming up with a plausible excuse for barging in on the ageing socialite, Macy closed her laptop, put on a pair of capris and a sunny yellow top and headed out the door, before she could talk herself out of it.

After asking at the hospital front desk how she might find the Volunteer Coordinator, Macy took the elevator up to the fourth floor and strode down the hall to the right, just like the nice lady at the information desk had told her to do. When she spotted the closed door clearly marked Volunteer Coordinator, she rapped on it sharply, stinging her knuckles in the process.

"Good heavens, you scared me to death!" Regina Risinger accused when she opened the door. "How can I help you?" she asked, not looking at all like she wanted to be of any kind of help whatsoever.

"Hi, I'm Macy Garson, may I come in?" Macy smiled, hoping to melt the older woman's frosty demeanor. If anything, her temperature dropped a few degrees more.

"I'm terribly busy…" Regina began, looking like she'd just tasted a particularly tart lemon.

"It won't take long, I promise." Macy crossed her fingers behind her back, hoping that she might be there a good long while.

"Fine, but this will have to be quick," Regina snipped. "I have a busy schedule. It's not like we take walk-ins. Have a seat." She nodded at a chair in front of her desk, which was painfully clean. Macy sat.

"Oh, you play tennis?" she asked innocently,

noticing a photo of Regina in tennis garb, holding a second-place trophy.

"I do. Can we please get to the point of your visit?" Her smile was like that of a python, full of cold, calculating strength. Macy swallowed.

"Yes, of course. I'm with Happy Paws, it's a non-kill shelter here in Danley, and I was wondering if the hospital might let us bring in some of the shelter pets to visit with patients."

The words had hardly left her lips when Regina snapped out a hard no.

"Out of the question. We have patients with allergies and shelter animals are notoriously unpredictable. There's also a hygiene issue. I'm sorry." Regina stood and looked pointedly at the door, which made Macy's blood boil. She'd met abused dogs who were nicer than this hag.

"Wow, sorry I asked. I noticed that one of our local librarians passed recently, maybe I should bring the animals there instead," she shot back, hoping for a reaction.

"Maybe what you should do is first, get out of my office, and second, mind your own business. Not everyone on the planet is an animal lover. Good day, Miss Garson."

"That went well," Macy muttered as she power

walked to the elevator and jabbed at the down button. She arrived on the ground floor out of breath and out of sorts.

Her phone had been buzzing in her purse with multiple notifications, and when she pulled it out to look at it, she was delighted to see that almost everything she'd listed from Lisa's jewelry collection had sold.

"Looks like I'll be able to pay for dinner tonight," she commented, tucking her phone back into the purse and heading home.

Macy had a horrific thought on the way home. What if the jewelry that she'd tucked away under the floorboards in her closet had been stolen? She'd have to refund the buyer and would undoubtedly lose her Super Seller status.

She hurried into the house and went straight to the closet, after locking the door behind her. She lifted the floorboard and peered down, holding her breath. The jewelry from Lisa's garage sale was still there. She released her breath in a rush and left it where it was. There would be a ton of packaging to do, and she didn't want to deal with it on an empty stomach. It would wait until after dinner.

In the meantime, she went online to search social

media for more garage and estate sales and found a promising one that began the next day.

"I can go to this one right after I finish my morning dog walking." She nodded, jotting down the address.

Her rather eventful day got the best of her, and Macy's intentions for packaging up Lisa's jewelry went out the window when she became immersed in a dog training documentary. She ordered a sub sandwich and a cookie for dinner and ate it while watching the show.

Her eyes grew heavier and heavier, and before she knew it, she was waking up to an entirely different show, her neck aching from falling asleep sitting up on the couch. It wasn't the first time since Jake passed that she'd let the television lull her to sleep, and it probably wouldn't be the last, but at least the dread of getting into a cold, empty bed was getting a bit easier to bear. Sometimes she still reached sleepily for him when she turned over during the night, only to be disappointed yet again. She was making progress. Spontaneous tears were mostly gone, and she could make it through most days without a gloomy cloud of despair hanging over her head.

Macy was thankful for the dogs and her human

friends at the shelter. They gave her something to focus on, and helped get her out of the house more often than she would have otherwise. She'd learned to smile again and was getting her sense of humor back too. Jake would have been proud. But then again, he always had been.

CHAPTER NINE

Essence was alone at the front counter of the shelter, busily clacking away at the computer keys, as usual.

"Morning," Macy greeted her.

"Hey, girl," Essence mumbled, clearly intent upon her task. "Sit in Polly's chair for a sec, I have news."

"Gotcha. Is everything okay? Is Polly…?"

Macy didn't even finish her sentence before Essence lifted one finger as a warning for her to be quiet, her eyes still glued to her computer screen.

"My bad, sorry," Macy whispered, causing Essence to shake her head as she completed whatever she was working on.

Essence tapped away until she finished, then hit one last key with finality, and spun in her chair to face Macy.

"What were you working on, national security?" Macy chuckled.

"I could tell you, but then I'd have to kill you," Essence shot back, examining her nails.

"So, you said you had news," Macy prompted.

"Yes, I do. My BFF Kenisha has a cousin named Nicco, and he's like this vocal coach," Essence began.

"Oh, I don't need a vocal coach," Macy protested with a chuckle. "I don't think there's any help for me in that regard."

Essence cocked an eyebrow and stared at her for a beat.

"Do you want to hear the news or not, Ms. Chatterbox?" she asked.

"Oh, I thought that was the news. Go on," Macy encouraged.

"Anyhow..." Essence gave her a warning glance before she continued. "Nicco is this voice coach—he's supposed to be pretty good, and pretty expensive—and guess who one of his favorite students is?" Essence smiled like the cat who ate the canary.

"Polly?" Macy guessed, mystified.

Essence rolled her eyes.

"Polly? Really? No, it's not Polly. It's your garage sale murder victim lady." Essence punctuated her sentence with a light clicking of neon pink nails on the desk.

"Oh!" Macy's eyes went wide.

"And that's not all." Essence leaned in, and Macy matched her. "Apparently, they were very ... close."

Macy's mouth dropped open with a sharp intake of breath. "No way!" she breathed.

"Way." Essence nodded.

"I wonder if he might be involved in the murder," Macy thought aloud.

"For Kenisha's family's sake, I hope not, but you never know." Essence pursed her lips.

"Well, at least my own ties to the situation will be done soon. I've sold almost all of her jewelry and will be shipping it out after I send it through the ionizer."

Essence shuddered. "Yes, girl, get that stuff out of your house like yesterday."

Macy was still thinking about the victim and the voice coach and garage sales in general while she walked a Corgi, a Schnauzer, and a pitiful-looking rat terrier whose huge eyes melted her heart. Leo the Great Dane was nowhere to be found, and she hoped that meant he'd gone for a walk with Polly or Sync.

Polly was back in her chair by the time that Macy returned from walking her furry friends, but she still didn't see Leo.

"Hey sunshine, how's it going?" Polly greeted her when she returned to the front.

"Good. Where's Leo?" Macy asked with a concerned frown.

"Leo was adopted late yesterday." Polly gave her a sympathetic smile.

"And the new owner was fiiiine!" Essence commented. "A doctor too."

"Awww… I'm glad he got a new home. He was a sweet boy," Macy replied, with a pang of sadness that she didn't get a chance to say goodbye.

"You should adopt a dog," Polly said, eyeing Macy. "They're good company you know."

"I have so much on my plate right now that I'm doing just fine loving on these dogs until they get new homes." Macy shook her head. "I'm not making any long-term plans right now, and a dog is a long-term commitment."

"We'll see how long that lasts." Polly chuckled. "I see the way you look at these poor orphans. It's only a matter of time before you take one or more of them home."

"We'll see about that." Macy headed for the door. "I'm headed for some garage sales. I'll be on the lookout for a No-No Nancy," she promised.

Essence shook her head and made a face.

"You do you, Boo."

"Jackpot," Macy murmured, driving home after visiting three particularly good garage sales.

She'd scored several valuable dolls, stuffed animals, and action figures, along with some vintage band t-shirts and sterling silverware.

After pulling into the driveway, she stepped gingerly through the yard, on the lookout for snakes, as she carried her bundles of treasure. Before she even set her bags and boxes down, Macy hurried through the kitchen to make sure that the back door was still securely locked, and only when she verified that it was, did she head down the hall to her guest room/inventory center.

Hydration came first, once she'd stacked her new items in the guest room, and then Macy settled in to clean and box up the jewelry and other items that had sold. She was proud of herself for making better choices and drinking water rather than diet soda, but as the day grew longer, and her neck began to hurt from craning it to make sure that every item was spotless and securely packaged, the more her resolve to make healthy choices waned. When at last she'd finished all of her tasks, she was tired and hungry enough that she simply hit the speed dial on her phone for pizza, rationalizing that she'd take longer walks with tomorrow's canines.

Her stomach growling, Macy grabbed the remote, flopped down onto the couch and turned on the TV. She planned to have a nice mellow evening and had no qualms about eating her dinner in front of the television. She'd worked hard and owed herself a relaxing evening of watching something she could follow without really needing to pay attention to it.

She'd just selected a ridiculous comedy to watch when the doorbell rang.

"Hi," she answered the door with a smile, anticipating the wonderfully gooey cheese, tomato sauce, and toppings on a slightly crunchy crust. She paused and stared for a moment at the delivery guy. He looked familiar, but she couldn't place him.

"Hi. I've got a veggie with pepperoni and extra mushrooms?" he said.

As soon as she heard his voice, Macy recognized him. Or so she thought. Could it really be the hitchhiker that she'd seen when she'd been lost in the country? His looks were pretty generic, so it was hard to tell.

"Yeah, that's what I ordered," she replied,

accepting the pizza. "Hey, have we met? Like, out in the country the other day? You look so familiar."

He froze and swallowed, then seemed to recover and pasted on a polite smile.

"No, I don't think so, but I get that a lot. Apparently, I just have one of those faces." He shrugged and turned to go. "Have a nice night."

Macy stared after him, frowning. He might or might not be the same guy that she saw, but he seemed to act oddly when she asked him about it.

"Girl, you need to stop jumping at shadows and being suspicious of everything and everyone. I need a hobby." She sighed and closed the door, heading to the couch.

CHAPTER TEN

Staring at the packages she'd wrapped up for the person who bought nearly all of the victim's jewelry, Macy's thoughts turned to the case again. It was like she couldn't help herself. She remembered what Essence had told her yesterday about the voice coach —Nicco was his name—who had been close to Lisa Greitz.

Macy had been thinking lately about the fact that she needed a hobby, and though she couldn't really afford it, maybe some voice lessons would be good for her. He'd earn every dime she paid him, that's for sure, and she might just be able to get some details from him that would be important to the case.

Nicco Sardinian wasn't very difficult to find online—he had quite a following on social media and seemed to document every moment of every day with smiles and drama-free content. He was also ridiculously handsome, in a dark, muscular, mysterious kind of way.

Her heart beating fast, her stomach all fluttery, just like it had been when she'd gone to visit the dragon, Regina Risinger, Macy called the number for Sing, Sing, Sing, Nicco's voice studio.

Nicco on the phone seemed to be just as nice as the image he projected on social media, which eased Macy's jitters a bit, though she still felt guilty for having ulterior motives.

"I have a cancellation this afternoon, at three, if you're available," he offered.

She could hear the smile in his tone. Maybe some of his carefree happiness would rub off on her.

"I'll be there, thanks," she replied, smiling without realizing it.

He was better looking in person than he was on social media, which Macy wouldn't have thought could be possible. He had a white-toothed movie star smile, a perfect tan, and looked dazzling in a pink v neck t-shirt and white linen shorts. He wore an interesting pendant on a gold chain around his neck and had a diamond stud in his left ear.

Macy guessed that they were about the same age,

which would hopefully make it easier to talk to him. He'd undoubtedly be a better conversationalist than Regina had been.

"So, how did you hear about me?" he asked, when they were perched, facing each other, atop stools in a small room lined with acoustical foam, an ancient piano pushed up against one wall.

"My friend Essence is friends with your cousin Kenisha." Macy figured honesty would be the best policy, because this man didn't seem like a murderer in the least bit.

"Oh, great!" He nodded enthusiastically. "I've met Essence. What a personality, and beautiful too. Breaks my heart that she won't go out with me." He clasped his hands dramatically over his heart and laughed.

"She's definitely a character." Macy chuckled. Her expression was grave when she spoke again. "So… I heard that you used to teach the librarian who … uh … died recently. Are you … okay?"

Nicco sobered for the first time as well and nodded.

"Yeah. It was a shock," he said in a hushed voice. "I couldn't imagine who could've done such a thing to such a sweet lady. She had the most beautiful voice." He shook his head and folded his arms in a manner that made his muscles bulge. Macy tried not to notice.

"Do you give lessons to a lady named Regina Risinger by any chance?" she asked, on a hunch.

"No, but it's strange that you would ask, because Lisa mentioned her more than once. Said that they'd had their disagreements on everything from Regina cheating at bridge to slamming tennis balls directly at her. She definitely didn't sound like someone I'd want to work with. I like positive people, you know? So anyway, should we get started?" he suggested, sitting up very straight, which made Macy follow suit.

"Yep, let's do this," she agreed, the muscles at the back of her neck tensing.

Her plan was to pretend to be horrible at singing so that she would have an excuse to either come back for more sessions, or quit, depending on how much information she thought that she could glean from Nicco.

After half an hour of instruction, he stared at her from his spot on the piano bench, at a loss.

"I think that I can help you," he began carefully, absently playing with the pendant at his throat. "But it's going to take some dedication on your part. Do you think you're up for the long haul?"

"Let me get back to you on that," Macy hedged.

"Finances are kind of tough for me right now, so I have to see if I can afford more lessons."

"No worries, I understand. First lesson is on the house." His look was so understanding that it made Macy feel even more guilty for her mild deception.

She was nearly halfway home when she realized why Nicco's pendant had fascinated her. Lisa Greitz had a pair of earrings that matched it, she realized with a start. She had just cleaned them that morning. Her heart thrumming, Macy also speculated that if she looked hard enough in the bottom of Lisa's jewelry box, she just might find the diamond earring that matched the one that Nicco had been wearing.

CHAPTER ELEVEN

"Holy heck, I never realized just how much of Jake's time was spent on mowing the silly lawn," Macy groused, dressed in cutoff sweatpants, one of Jake's old t-shirts, and steel toed boots, because … snakes.

She had already stashed the packages that needed to go to the post office in the bottom of her closet so that she could address them later, and if she had time after mowing and a shower, she'd get them mailed off, good riddance. In the meantime, Lisa Greitz's jewelry was at least out of sight and ready to go, except of course for the jewelry box and other things that were under the floorboards.

Noting that finishing up a cup of coffee was a perfectly legitimate means of procrastination, she refilled her mug and took a healthy gulp as she leaned against the kitchen counter, glaring balefully out at the ever-growing lawn. She'd do the backyard today, and by the time tomorrow rolled around, it'd be time to do the dreaded front yard again. It was an endless cycle.

Just as she raised the mug to her lips to savor the last sip, a loud pounding at the front door startled her. When she jumped, the mug tipped and dumped the dregs of coffee down the front of her shirt.

"Whoever you are, you're lucky that this is an old shirt," she grumbled, grabbing a kitchen towel on the way to the door and trying to mop up the worst of it by dabbing at the well-worn fabric.

Beyond annoyed, she yanked open the door and froze when she came face to face with the two deputies who came to see her during the breaking and entering snake fiasco.

Mortified at her appearance, Macy tried to manufacture a smile.

"Hey. Have you found the intruder?" she asked, hopefully.

Mountain and Teapot stared at her, and finally, Teapot—the one in her mind that she'd assigned the role of bad cop to—spoke.

"You were at a garage sale a few weeks ago and

bought several items from a woman named Lisa Greitz," he began, his tone dark.

Macy's heart skipped a beat, and she willed herself not to flush a nervous red.

"Yeah, I saw on the news that she'd been murdered. So awful," she replied.

"You know her before the garage sale?" Teapot asked.

"No. I'm new to the area, so I don't really know very many people at all yet."

"What items did you buy from the victim?" Mountain chimed in.

"Umm… I'm not sure of all of them, but I bought some toys and some jewelry, I know that much."

"Isn't it true that you bought all of the jewelry that she had for sale that day?" Teapot challenged, hitching at his belt.

"Yes, I did." Macy nodded, wondering where he was going with all of this and not liking one bit the suspicious look in his eyes.

"And where is that jewelry now?" Teapot asked, more of an accusation than a question.

"All of it sold," Macy answered truthfully. It *had* sold, at least most of it. They didn't ask her specifically if she had taken it to the post office yet.

"Mind if we come in and take a look?" Mountain

asked. His tone wasn't exactly friendly, but it wasn't as harsh as his partner's.

Macy licked her lips and squared her shoulders. All those years of watching crime dramas on TV were finally about to pay off.

"You got a warrant for that?" she asked with a level gaze, channeling every clever criminal she'd ever seen on television. *Take that, mean coppers!*

Teapot's flush started at his too-tight collar and crept up to his neck and ears.

"No, we don't, and with that attitude of yours, you've just become a person of interest in a murder case," he growled, a sheen of sweat breaking out on his forehead and upper lip.

That never happened in the crime shows...

Macy gaped at him like a fish out of water, stunned to her core. A murder suspect? Her? She had once nearly fainted during an autopsy scene on one of her favorite shows. Dead bodies were definitely not on her list of things that she could handle.

"Look," Mountain interrupted, his tone more reasonable. "If you have nothing to hide, then there's nothing to worry about. Just let us in to have a look, and then we'll be on our way."

Nauseated, Macy nodded and stepped back so that

they could enter. She trailed after them as they went from room to room.

"Did any of this stuff belong to the victim?" Teapot asked, when they crowded into what little space was left in the guest room.

"No." She shook her head vehemently.

She reasoned that if the police were so off base that they had added her to the suspect list, then she'd have no choice but to track down the perpetrator herself. And technically, he hadn't asked her about the items that were boxed up and in the closet, so she was being truthful when she said that none of the stuff that was out in plain sight had belonged to the victim.

"You know ... charges of this nature can really ruin a business venture," Teapot said with a nasty smile.

Macy swallowed hard. She'd finally found a way to make a living, and she wasn't about to let some rotund cop with a bad attitude knock her off course.

"Understandable," she replied, her eyes like granite.

They trudged through the rest of the house, with Teapot making a big show of looking in every nook and cranny—*yes, Officer, I'm hiding the murder weapon in my medicine cabinet*—and eventually went on their way with a stern warning to Macy that she should let them know anything that she remembered from her one-time encounter with Lisa Greitz that might help them in their investigation.

She glared at them as they drove away, then stomped through the house and into the garage to get the mower. She attacked the back yard with a vengeance, fuming—snakes be darned. Even the little reptilian demons couldn't deter her today.

On her fourth trip across the back lawn, Macy saw a small movement out of the corner of her eye, and her heart leapt to her throat as she dropped the handle to the mower and skittered sideways in her steel-toed boots.

Scrambling to scale and stand atop the air conditioner, she stared at the corner of the deck where she thought she saw motion and sagged with relief when she saw a tiny grey paw dart out, batting at a piece of grass.

Her heart still thumping in her chest, Macy climbed down from the air conditioner and moved in for a closer look. When her steel-toed boots stopped by the corner of the deck, she heard a pitiful mew coming from below the graying wooden planks.

Oh no. No way. That is the last thing I need in my life right now.

The sky clouded over, and a loud thunderclap made Macy jump.

"Seriously?" Exasperated, she turned her face skyward and shook her head.

Fully aware of what was about to happen, Macy dragged the mower to the tiny garden shed and stashed it there. As she dashed back toward the house, she again heard a tiny mew. It was a sound that cut straight through any semblance of rationality and went straight to her heart. Standing there as the first drops of rain began to splat all around her, Macy sighed, squatted down, and bravely reached under the deck, grabbing a small, squirmy kitten. Tucking it against her body, she ran into the house, just as the skies opened.

CHAPTER TWELVE

After making sure that the sweet and seemingly mellow kitten was warm and dry, Macy put her in a giant cardboard box with a baking pan full of kitty litter, that had been left in the garage by the previous owner, in one end, and a pile of fluffy towels in the other end. She took the box, kitten and all, into the guest room with her and retrieved the victim's jewelry box from beneath the floorboards.

After placing a stuffed animal in the kitten's box to keep her company, Macy painstakingly took every piece of jewelry out of Lisa Greitz's jewelry box.

Her breath caught in her throat when she found not only the earrings that matched the pendant that Nicco had been wearing, but the matching diamond stud as well.

"Why would she sell something so valuable in a garage sale?" Macy wondered aloud. The kitten mewed a response from deep inside the box, but Macy was so lost in her thoughts that she barely heard it. "Must be a fake, right?"

Frowning, she put the unsold items back into the jewelry box, stashing it once again under the floorboards. When she went to address the items in the bottom of the closet that she'd already boxed up, Macy scanned the list of addresses on VendMore and noticed something odd. Several of the items had been bought by someone who was sending them to the victim's address.

Who would do such a thing? Her rival maybe? But how would the rival know where to find the victim's jewelry? Stymied, Macy sat in the doorway of the closet, wondering what on earth to do. Should she not send those boxes and tell the police? They hadn't seemed to view her in a very positive light, so that was a no.

Ultimately, she decided to do some sleuthing and see if she could find out some information about the buyer, which ended up only making her more frustrated. Her store account listed the buyer as a visitor and the profile picture was blank. There was no information as to where they lived or how they had paid.

The buyer had requested that the items be gift wrapped.

Who would send the victim's jewelry to her husband, gift wrapped? Wouldn't that be a bit like rubbing salt into a wound? As only a rival or jilted lover could do…?

Maybe Lisa was having an affair and had broken things off with Nicco, which is why she disposed of the jewelry that matched his at the garage sale.

Macy's stomach rumbled with hunger which made her think of the pizza guy/hitchhiker. Had it been mere coincidence that he'd been in the middle of nowhere just when she'd been looking for a garage sale? What had been in his backpack, she wondered, her blood running cold. And who was the guy in the grocery store who had given her the address?

There was one way that she could think of to get some answers, and that meant signing up for more voice lessons.

CHAPTER THIRTEEN

"Are you going to stay put and behave?" Macy asked the tiny kitten, who gazed back up at her with big blue eyes and opened her mouth in a silent mew.

"Uh-huh. I know you look harmless and adorable right now, but I've seen the carnage that a cat left to its own devices can inflict."

She had given the kitten a small saucer of milk and planned to stop at the grocery store on the way home to buy a bag and some cans of kitten chow.

"I'm going to find you a good home as soon as I can, little girl," Macy cooed, scratching the purring kitten between the ears. "So don't get too comfortable here," she warned, her heart warming as the tiny creature batted at her hand when she withdrew it. "And stop being so darn cute. I'm impervious to cuteness. It won't work. Many dogs have tried and failed."

Macy put the box with the fluffy towels and kitty litter, which to her surprise and delight, the kitten had actually used, in the bathroom, and leaving the light on, she shut the door, just in case the kitten developed superpowers and jumped out of the box while she was gone.

She'd been able to secure another last-minute appointment with Nicco and was a bit terrified to go see him this time. He was wearing jewelry given to him by a woman who was now dead. Murdered, in fact. Had he been the vindictive lover who'd made arrangements to mail her jewelry back to her own home? Macy was determined to find out and hoped that she'd live to tell the tale. Whenever the main character in a crime show makes the perpetrator angry, it doesn't go well for them.

At least on TV, the main character usually has a partner or significant other who comes in to rescue them at the last second. Macy didn't have that luxury. Her significant other was gone, and the local cops would just as soon blame her for the crime and be done with it. So, no matter what, she couldn't mess this meeting up. The consequences could be dire.

Psyching herself up, Macy had gone to great

lengths to tamp down her panic as she drove to Sing, Sing, Sing. It turned out that she needn't have worried. When she pulled into the parking lot, an extremely attractive man was leaving the studio. Nicco said something to him from the doorway, and he laughed, trotted back up the steps, and kissed Nicco on the cheek before embracing him warmly.

"Ohhhh…" Macy murmured, realization dawning. "I guess he didn't have an affair with Lisa after all," she concluded. "But then … where and why did he get the jewelry? One way to find out, I guess."

No longer terrified, she got out of the car and entered the building. She'd still be careful, but now Macy was thinking that Nicco might just make a really good ally.

"Great to see you again," he grinned, opening his arms for a hug.

Surprised, Macy let him enfold her, and the impact of feeling strong arms hugging her was immediate. Her eyes welled with tears, and she pulled away.

"Oh no! What's the matter, Miss Macy?" Nicco asked, holding her by the shoulders, his deep brown eyes alarmed.

"I'm sorry," Macy choked out, feeling like a fool. "It's just … my husband died a few months ago and I don't… I don't really get hugs much anymore," she admitted, her heart breaking at the realization.

"Oh sweetie … come here," Nicco said gently.

He held her while she cried. Sobs shook her shoulders, and she buried her face in his clean-smelling silk, flamingo-print shirt.

"That's right … let it all out," he murmured against her hair, rubbing her upper arm to soothe her.

"I'm sorry…" she gasped, her breath coming in hitches and bursts.

"Nothing to be sorry for. It's okay. You're safe," he promised, and oddly, she believed him.

When the storm had passed, Macy pulled away and wiped her eyes, taking a big sniff in.

"Thanks, I guess I needed that, even if I didn't know it," she smiled wanly.

"I'm told I give very good hugs, so I'm here for you when you need me. I mean that." Nicco squeezed her arm and let go. "Do we need to reschedule your lesson?"

Macy shook her head.

"No. I don't know how great my voice will be at the moment, but I think it would be a good way to help me focus on something positive."

"You got it," Nicco agreed, going to the studio's interior door and holding it open for her.

"Thanks," Macy gave him a bit stronger smile this time, and perched on her stool, while he headed for the piano.

"We did vocal exercises and scales last time, but today is a different day and maybe we need to change things up a bit. Let's start with a song. Any requests?" Nicco asked.

"I like Mariah Carey…"

Nicco stared at her for a moment. "Mariah Carey. That's pretty … ambitious. You sure you want to lead with that?" His brows rose.

"Yep, let's do this." Macy nodded, taking in a deep, shuddering breath. It was time to reveal her secret.

She recognized the opening notes of one of her favorite songs, and when Nicco nodded his head, indicating that she should start, she sang, closing her eyes and pretending that she was in the shower.

She missed the stunned look on Nicco's face, that evolved into an amazed grin. When he played the last note and she exhaled, opening her eyes, he burst into spontaneous applause.

"Where did that come from?" he demanded, clearly pleased.

"You're a great teacher, and I've been practicing,"

Macy said shyly, feeling her face heat up at his genuine praise.

"Okay, Macy... I may be a pretty good teacher, but that voice is not something that you learned. That's all you. You've been holding out on me," he accused, smiling and shaking his finger at her.

"Actually ... I have," Macy confessed, squirming a bit.

Nicco sobered. "Oh?" he asked, puzzled.

"Yeah, the first time that I came here... I didn't really come for the lesson," Macy admitted.

"Oh, I think you might have the wrong idea..." Nicco began, looking embarrassed.

"No, no, definitely not that. I saw your boyfriend leave when I drove up," Macy smiled. "Believe me, now that I'm a widow, I don't think that I'll ever date again. But I did come here with an ulterior motive."

Nicco frowned but said nothing.

"Remember how I asked you about Lisa Greitz? Well, the reason that I did is that I thought you might be able to help me find who killed her."

In for a penny, in for a pound. With that single statement, she put her trust in her instincts. The instincts that told her that Nicco was not a murderer. Hopefully, she was right.

"I met Lisa right before she ... died. I was at her

garage sale and bought a bunch of things. I have an online store at VendMore, and shortly after the sale, I listed a bunch of her jewelry. Someone bought almost all of it, which I understood, because it was high-quality stuff that was in really great shape. But ... when I packaged it all up and checked the address on the order, whoever ordered the items wanted them to be shipped back to Lisa's address," Macy explained.

"That's weird. Why would someone do that?" Nicco mused.

"That's what I wondered. The only person that came to mind was Regina Risinger. Was their rivalry enough to make her that vindictive? Could she have killed her and just want to now throw salt in the wound by sending her things back to her house?" Macy thought aloud.

She neglected to point out that Regina hadn't actually been her only suspect. Nicco had been on the list as well until she discovered that he couldn't have been having an affair with the victim.

Nicco nodded slowly. "Yeah, I could see Regina being the one. There was definitely no love lost between the two of them. Everyone liked Lisa because she was kind and giving. It seemed like Regina just wanted the press and trophies. At least that's what Lisa thought of her."

"Have you ever talked to Lisa's husband?" Macy asked.

"Definitely not. Someone started a rumor that Lisa and I were having an affair, which cracks me up, considering the circumstances. But, I never wanted to intrude in her personal life, just in case people actually believed the rumor."

"Yeah, that makes sense. I just think that whoever was mailing the jewelry back to Lisa's house was doing an unnecessarily cruel thing to her husband. Can you imagine how he'd feel receiving that?" Macy shook her head.

"Yeah, Lisa used to glow when she talked about him, so he has to be devastated at her death. Poor guy."

"Well, maybe we can figure out who the killer is so that he can have some closure," Macy commented.

"Shouldn't the police be the ones doing that?" Nicco said gently.

"If they hadn't accused me of being involved, I might trust them to do that." Macy's mouth was set in a firm line.

CHAPTER FOURTEEN

Macy was going to find a home for the kitten, she really was, but in the meantime, she figured that it would be best to get an actual litter box, some cute little food bowls with fishies embossed on the bottom, an assortment of cat toys, and an upgraded version of kitten food. She wanted the cute little stinker to be healthy and happy when she went to her new home. Which would be soon.

She twitched a tuft of feathers attached to the end of a stick back and forth, making the kitten dart after it, batting at it with tiny fluffy paws, while she drank her coffee and munched on a bran muffin. She was trying to eat more healthy foods and figured that bran muffins were a step up from the chocolate chocolate chip ones that she usually favored.

"Oh geez," Macy exclaimed, glancing at her phone and seeing the time. She'd spent more than half an hour entertaining her tiny house guest. "Okay, I need to do something with Lisa Greitz's jewelry, but I have to find out who the mystery buyer is," she thought aloud.

Though the buyer's identity was hidden from her on the VendMore app, there was a little icon that indicated that she could message them.

"Oh, I know!" Her heart sped up as she figured out a potential way to draw them out. She opened the message center and tapped out a message.

Hi there! I noticed that your destination address is local. Would you like me to deliver the items personally? It would be much faster than sending them through the mail, and I'd be happy to return your shipping charges.

She hit send, and it wasn't twenty seconds later that she received a reply.

Absolutely not. The recipient is battling an illness and should not be disturbed.

Macy was stumped. If the buyer was Regina Risinger, why wouldn't she want the items delivered as soon as possible? Was it possible that she had murdered Lisa's husband as well and was sending the jewelry back to their house as some sort of odd message for the police?

Macy had a sudden urge to drive over to Lisa's house immediately to see if there was anything suspicious going on, but prudence won out. She really didn't have anything to go on, and if she knocked on the door and Lisa's husband answered, she'd have some explaining to do that might just get her reported to the police, and she'd had more than enough of their company lately.

Still pondering the case as she boxed up new orders that thankfully had nothing to do with Lisa Greitz, Macy remembered the pizza guy. Had it really been just a coincidence that he happened to be hitchhiking near the spot in the country that she'd been sent to on a wild goose chase? With all the strange things that had been happening to her lately, Macy was disinclined to think so.

If it wasn't just a coincidence, who was the pizza guy and why had he been out in the middle of nowhere? She was determined to find out. After two more hours of boxing up orders, Macy glanced at her watch. 1:00. Her favorite pizza place had been delivering for over an hour now, so she took a chance and pulled out her phone.

Hi, this is Macy Garson. I'd like to order my usual

—you can put it on the card that I have on file—and is it possible to have the same delivery person that I had last time? He did such a good job that I'd like to give him a really nice tip. Oh, you can? Perfect—thanks so much!

Macy hung up the phone with a triumphant smile, which faded when she realized that she had completed only the easiest part of her scheme. Now she'd actually have to confront the man who might or might not have been involved in setting up her misguided little adventure in the countryside.

When the doorbell rang, roughly twenty minutes later, she smoothed down her hair, rubbed her palms on the back of her denim shorts, strode bravely to the door, and flung it open before her nerves could get the best of her.

"Hi there, I've got a veggie with…" the delivery guy began.

"I know you," Macy interrupted, staring him down. She had recognized him immediately this time.

"Ummm … what?" The guy half smiled, but his eyes showed uncertainty.

Please don't let him be a serial killer…

"You were hitchhiking out in the middle of nowhere and asked me for a ride. Why were you out there? If you're a delivery guy, that means you have to have a car, and if you have a car, you wouldn't have been hitchhiking," Macy blurted, folding her arms.

He laughed nervously and cleared his throat when he tried to speak but only emitted a squeak. He tried again, shaking his head.

"I'm sorry, lady. I don't know what you're talking about, but your pizza is going to get cold if you don't..." he began, taking the pizza out of the warming bag.

"Yes, you do know what I'm talking about," Macy accused, snatching the pizza from him. If he bolted, she wanted to make sure she had her pizza first. "And if you don't fess up and explain yourself, I'll call your boss and tell him that you ate some of my pizza before you delivered it," she threatened.

Maybe he was a serial killer or maybe he wasn't, but either way, she'd probably already ticked him off, so why be shy now?

The guy stared at her for a moment, shifting his weight from one foot to the other, then cast a glance skyward and sighed.

"Look, it was really no big deal." He grimaced and let the empty warming back droop down by his side. "This guy that I delivered a pizza to asked me if I wanted to make some extra money. I'm not exactly a high roller, ya know? So I asked him what I needed to do for it. Thought he might offer me a side gig or something. So he tells me that all I have to do is stand behind some trees and let him know by text when you pulled up, looking lost."

Macy's blood ran cold. This definitely sounded dangerous. Her instinct to run away when the pizza guy asked for a ride may have saved her life. "That's it?" she asked, trying to sound nonchalant.

"No. He also said that if you gave me a ride, that I should have you drop me off at a barn down the road. He said that you were his daughter, and he was going to surprise you with a new horse."

If Macy wasn't so food conscious, she was pretty sure she'd have dropped the pizza box at that point, when an icy chill shuddered through her.

"Did you ever go to the barn, even though I drove off?" she asked, determined to be brave and not clue the guy into her suspicions.

"No, but the guy gave me directions there, because he thought you would pick me up."

"Give me the directions," Macy demanded, her fear evolving into fury.

"I'll give 'em to you, but you can't tell him where you got them," the pizza guy countered. "He paid pretty well, and I could use a gig like that every now and then."

"I'll make you a deal. I won't tell him how I got the directions, if you don't let on that I know what happened," Macy offered.

"Works for me." The pizza guy shrugged.

"Do you know his name?" Macy asked.

"No, but *you* should. I mean, I know *my* dad's name," he snickered.

"Do you remember what address you delivered his pizza to?" Macy ignored the jibe.

"No way. I go so many places every day. They're all a blur." He shrugged.

"Fine." Macy sighed, pulled a crumpled bill out of her shorts pocket and handed it to him.

"Thank you, have a nice night," the guy gave her a fake smile and hurried back to his car.

"Remember our deal!" Macy called after him.

The info that she'd gleaned was pretty disturbing, but at least she'd gotten a pizza out of it.

CHAPTER FIFTEEN

"So apparently, there is something to that old saying that curiosity killed the cat," Macy observed, using one hand to scoop up the curious kitten who was currently bunking with her. She relocated the wiggling mini feline to a spot where she wouldn't have to fight off perusing paws while trying to solve a mystery.

Macy was sitting on the floor in the guest room, going through all the remaining items that she had left from Lisa Greitz's collection, and the mewing menace took every opportunity to play with each shiny object that her perpetually darting blue eyes discovered. She batted at necklaces and bit at earrings. She sat staring at a rhinestone encrusted ring, the tip of her tail twitching back and forth, eventually pouncing on it.

Her paws, with their needle-sharp claws that she still didn't quite know how to control, were always busy finding something new and interesting to play with. She made Macy laugh out loud more than once, despite herself.

The kitten was a welcome diversion from the dark possibilities that had been worrying Macy all morning. She'd left her voice lesson yesterday determined to get to the bottom of whatever was going on, even if that meant putting herself in danger. For all she knew, she might be next on the killer's list as it was.

She planned to deliver the jewelry items that had been purchased personally, even though the buyer had told her not to. If there was a body to be discovered, so be it. She shuddered at the thought, and refused to even consider how the police would feel about her being the one who reported yet another casualty.

Macy had plugged in her old canister vacuum, and had removed the attachment at the end, so that she could just use the hose to remove some of the dust that had accumulated in the bottom of the jewelry box.

When the hose sucked at the bottom of the box's interior, the light blue velvet lining loosened, threatening to be sucked up into oblivion. Macy hurriedly hit the off switch on the vacuum and when she examined the interior of the box to survey the damage, she was astonished to find a secret compartment beneath the delicate lining.

Her heart rate accelerating, Macy reached into the box and pulled out a folded and yellowed piece of paper. There was an address on the paper that sounded vaguely familiar, but she couldn't quite place it. Remembering another mystery from Lisa's jewelry box, Macy pulled out the tiny photo from the golden locket, and placed it face down, so that she could see the series of numbers on the back.

Try as she might, while fending off the kitten with her free hand, Macy couldn't seem to tie the address with the numbers in any way. Feeling as though she was intruding in the personal life of a dead woman, she shuddered and tried to think of a safe place to put those particular items until she could figure out what they meant. She settled on slipping them into the empty space behind the drawer in her nightstand. Macy felt sort of silly about the cloak and dagger routine, but she figured that, just in case someone with ill intent came looking for them, they'd be safely tucked away.

An idea struck her right after she secured the mysterious items, and she hurriedly scrolled through her phone.

"I knew it!" she breathed, eyes going wide.

The address that the pizza guy had given her matched the address that was in the jewelry box! It was clearly a rural location, as evidenced by the series of numbers and directionals.

"I have to go out there, that's all there is to it," Macy decided, her stomach fluttering with nervous butterflies. "Okay Miss Kitty-Cat, you're going to have to exist on your own for a little while. I have to go visit an address that was given to me from beyond the grave."

She stilled, hearing her own words, and swallowed hard. Taking a deep breath and shaking off the major case of the willies that she'd just given herself, Macy scooped up the cat and left the guest room, closing the door behind her. She'd taken to closing all of the doors in the house whenever she had to leave, just to minimize the chances of the kitten getting into mischief while she was away.

Jake's basketball shorts and a loose tank top with a picture of a burger on it seemed like a poor choice of clothing when one was potentially heading out to meet their doom, so Macy donned a pair of capris that she had to suck in her tummy to fasten, and a pink polo shirt because pink was her favorite color and she needed as much of an emotional boost as she could get. Though they looked a bit strange with her capris, she chose snow-white running shoes—that obviously had never been used for running—with thin white ankle socks. She might have to make a quick getaway, so she could at least have the proper footwear for it.

When she sat in the driver's seat of her car, Macy nearly chickened out, but when she considered the fact that Teapot and Mountain had put her on their persons of interest list, she gritted her teeth and turned the ignition over. Whether she wanted to or not, she had to get to the bottom of Lisa Greitz's untimely death. Her own survival might just depend on it.

She plugged the address into her GPS and followed the instructions that led her outside the city limits, as she suspected, to a rural area that was quite close to where the garage sale was supposed to have been. Macy pulled over to the side of the road, her A/C on full blast to combat sweat that was a product both of the heat and her jangled nerves.

"There's literally nothing here," she mumbled, her eyes scanning the brush that was thick on both sides of the narrow country road. "Oh, wait…" Her breath caught. Just past the nose of the car, but on the other side of the road, was a spot in the brush that looked like it might be concealing a path.

"Do or die," Macy muttered, getting out of the car

and wincing at the loud bang her door made when she closed it. "So much for stealth." She sighed, then, out of habit, hit the button on her key fob to lock the car.

"I was right," she said out loud, the sound of her voice making her feel somehow less alone.

There was indeed a path that led through the brush. She couldn't see what was at the end of it, and it looked like she might be attacked by sticks, thorns, and assorted wildlife if she ventured down it, but Macy decided that she'd come too far to turn back now.

"This thing goes on forever," she grumbled, trudging along and swatting away impressive clouds of gnats and mosquitos the size of small airplanes. The thought crossed her mind that she was getting farther and farther from her car and civilization. No one was around to hear ... anything. Even a scream.

She rounded a bend in the path and was confronted by a small creek that looked like it was probably teeming with unsafe microbes.

"Ewww..." Macy grimaced. "There's no way I'm walking through that."

It appeared to be just narrow enough that she might be able to jump it, though her creek-jumping skills were admittedly more than a bit rusty.

Backing up so that she could get a running start, Macy felt a surge of adrenaline burst through her.

"One, two, threeee..." she ran at the creek and launched herself in the air. The ground below her seemed to roll by in slow motion as she saw that she was going to clear the water. Unfortunately, what she hadn't planned on was just how boggy the bank of the creek was on the other side. Her feet hit it with a smothering splat, and she immediately sank in up to her ankles.

"Really? My white shoes?" she groaned, wiping dribbles of mud from her upper thighs and flinging them from her fingertips.

Exasperated, she lifted her left foot out of the muck and placed it on much more stable land. When she lifted her right foot, her formerly white sock made an appearance, but her right shoe stayed mired in place, nearly making her topple over onto the bank.

"Are you kidding me right now?" she blurted, watching in horror as the mud enveloped her shoe, seeming to suck it into an abyss.

Something skittered in the bushes to her right, and Macy seriously contemplated leaving the shoe right where it was, but then realized that encountering things with fangs would probably be much better with some foot protection.

Keeping her left foot on firm ground, Macy stretched toward the spot where her shoe had disappeared.

"Oh, eww eww eww…" Plunging her hand into the mud, her face contorted in disgust, she felt around in the goo until her fingers grazed something solid. Keeping an eye out for any slithering creatures that might be planning an ambush, she grasped the shoe, grunting, tugging, and willing it to pull free.

"Come on!" she growled, tugging with all of her might.

She leaned into it, leveraging her body weight against the apparently powerful grip of the mud.

"Come. On!" she grunted again, giving one final heave backward.

The shoe gave suddenly, freeing itself and her hand slipped back up through the mud so fast that the momentum threw her backward. Her rump hit the bank with a thud, and mud flew into the air, raining down into her hair and onto her clothes.

"Perfect." Macy nodded, holding her mud-filled shoe up and tipping it over to empty it. The mud clung to the shoe as if for dear life, and she had to reach into it with her other hand to scoop out the muck. "Why am I doing this, again?" she grumbled, shuddering as she slipped her foot back into the heavy wetness of the shoe.

Her trudging now had a cadence to it, slap, squelch, slap, squelch, and an unpleasant, earthy odor emanated from her shoes.

"I don't even want to know what kinds of bacteria I've been exposed to," she muttered, slapping at perhaps the hundredth mosquito who buzzed next to her ear.

She itched from head to toe, with bug bites both real and imagined, her feet and legs ached from the walk through hostile terrain, and the wisps of hair that had come loose from her ponytail clung to her forehead, neck, back, and face. Her persistence paid off, however, when she reached a large barn that looked like she could easily push it over with the slightest touch.

"Well, there's the barn. Where's my birthday pony?" she murmured, staring at the ancient looking structure. "Do I really want to see what's in there?"

Everything, from the mosquito bites to the mud-soaked shoes would be a colossal waste if she turned back now. Heaving another deep sigh, she strode toward the open set of doors.

Expecting a cobweb-filled nightmare, Macy was puzzled to discover that the barn floor was spotless.

"How on earth did it stay this way after all these years," she wondered aloud, scanning the cavernous space. "There has to be something significant here or this address wouldn't have been tucked so carefully away in Lisa's jewelry box."

Saying the victim's name in the abandoned barn, in the middle of nowhere made her shiver, despite the stillness and heat.

When she saw what looked like a storage closet in the corner, Macy was drawn to it like a moth to a flame.

"If I was looking for a hiding spot for something important, this is the first place I'd choose," she reasoned, opening the door. "Of course. The rest of the barn is spotless, and this one room is filthy. Great."

Waving a hand to move the cobwebs out of the way, Macy moved into the room, bent down, tapped at different spots on the floor, and discovered that one of the floorboards was loose.

"Oh man, this could either be good or it could be writhing with spiders and snakes," she muttered trying to pry up the board. "Or maybe I've just seen Indiana Jones too many times."

Bracing herself and wiggling her fingers underneath the small gap between planks, she finally lifted the loose board and set it aside. Her heart leapt when she spotted a box in the space between the joists in the floor. Grabbing the piece of paper that was on top of the box, she shoved it in her pocket so that she could see what was in the box and hightail it out of the creepy barn.

The paper was apparently covered with dust and Macy sneezed, the sound echoing in the room.

"Gristle County Sheriff's Department. Freeze! Put your hands behind your head, slowly stand, and walk backward toward me," a rough voice ordered, scaring the life out of her. "You're under arrest for breaking and entering, theft, and murder."

CHAPTER SIXTEEN

Macy's teeth chattered as a torrent of emotions crashed through her. She'd never been in a police car before, and she didn't know if her terror over being arrested was more profound than her anger at the officers for not speaking with her or allowing her to explain. They also had the air-conditioning in the police car set too low, so that certainly didn't help with the chattering.

"Hey!" she called out, anger finally winning the battle over terror. "You really need to let me explain why I was out there in that horrible barn."

No response.

Macy tried to lean forward far enough to bang her head on the plexiglass partition that separated her from the stone-faced officers, but the seatbelt wouldn't allow it, and the more she tried, the tighter it got.

"Seriously, will you at least listen to me?" she hollered.

They didn't even glance in her direction.

Tears of frustration, fear, and anger, with a little self-pity thrown in for good measure, threatened to fall, but Macy was determined that under no circumstances would she give them the satisfaction of seeing her cry.

When the cruiser finally came to a stop at the station, she thought she'd finally have a chance to explain, but they silenced her with steely looks when she tried, so she just went silent. They'd have to let her speak eventually, so she made up her mind to just be quiet until they did.

She was led to an interrogation room which looked much like the ones that she'd seen on TV. It was a surreal experience. Mountain took off the zip-tie that had been keeping her hands behind her back, and Macy rubbed her wrists, shooting a glare at him.

"Sit," Teapot ordered, nodding to a single metal chair that was bolted to the floor on one side of a matching table.

He and Mountain sat in two folding chairs on the other side, facing her. Their expressions weren't in the least bit reassuring. As they stared at her, she finally got a chance to look at their name badges. Mountain was actually Officer Moran, and Teapot was Officer Beadles. That one almost made her giggle for reasons that she couldn't quite fathom in her present circumstances.

"You're going to start from the beginning, and you're going to tell us everything," Moran ordered.

He'd been the kinder of the two officers in their previous encounters, but he clearly had no empathy for Macy at that moment.

Macy clenched her teeth, her eyes narrowing at the unfairness of her predicament.

"You want to know everything? Fine. I'll tell you everything, because I think I've actually figured out more about this case than you have. If you're going to be obtuse enough to suspect me when there is so much suspicious stuff going on right under your noses, then yeah, I'll tell you everything, and when I'm done, I expect an apology," she seethed.

Moran raised an eyebrow at her. Beadle yawned. Their utter lack of reaction deflated her bravado, and she sighed.

When the floodgates of information opened, Macy didn't hold anything back. She told them about the jewelry that Nicco wore, and that he wasn't having an affair with Lisa Greitz. She told them about how nasty Regina Risinger was and how she and Lisa were rivals in everything. She told them about the numbers on the back of the photo from the locket, and about how the man in the grocery store, who had given her an address in the middle of nowhere, had hired a pizza guy to lure her to the barn, but that she'd driven away. Feeling utterly spent after the purging of her soul, Macy fell silent, staring at the table and wishing that she had an extra-large diet soda, with lime.

"Anything else?" Mountain asked.

"Oh, I almost forgot." Macy reached into her pocket and pulled out the piece of paper that she had taken from the space under the floor in the barn.

"What's that?" Teapot demanded.

"I have no idea. I found it in the storage room where you so rudely interrupted me. Let me read it," Macy snapped, her patience at an end.

"Arthur, if you find this, it's because you've done something horrific to me. Don't think I don't know where your true loyalties lie. I set up this location as a decoy and told Regina Risinger about it, and the combination numbers in my locket, to see if it would get back to you. She's probably as guilty as you are. If so, I hope you both get what you deserve, which doesn't include my inheritance. My attorney has my will and a copy of the address where my actual lockbox is located, in a bank, where people always keep their prized possessions. You know what the sad thing is, Arthur? I actually loved you … for a while. Then you were just an ill-advised habit that I couldn't seem to break. I've left all of my money to the children's hospital in Jacksonville. I'm hoping that whoever ends up with my jewelry box and locket will find this before you do and will expose you for the shameless money-grubber that you are. Shame on you, Arthur. From the grave I say, Shame. On. You!"

Moran and Beadle exchanged a glance and seemed to be actively avoiding Macy's gaze. Another uniformed officer knocked briefly on the door and entered, beckoning for Moran and Beadle to join him in the back of the room.

Macy strained to overhear the conversation, while trying to appear to ignore them completely. She didn't hear everything, but she heard enough to get the gist of what they were being told, and she breathed a sigh of relief.

The murder weapon and some bloodstained clothing was found near the property, along with lots of fingerprints that belonged to Arthur Greitz. While sad for Lisa, Macy was glad that there had at least been some closure to the case, and that the killer, her husband, would wind up behind bars, where he belonged, along with his sidekick Regina.

The officer left, and Moran and Beadle turned toward Macy with the look of two men who had recently consumed a fair helping of crow.

"See, told you it wasn't me," she commented, folding her arms and giving them a look.

"Come on, we'll show you the way out." Moran inclined his head toward the door, while Beadle just stared at her, his mouth puckered like he'd been sipping lemon juice.

As they led Macy out of the interrogation room, she heard a ruckus farther down the hall and peeked down that way from behind Moran's considerable bulk.

"That's the guy from the grocery store," she whispered, feeling faint at first, but then furious.

When two officers muscled him past, Macy spoke before even making up her mind as to whether or not she should.

"You! You knew I had the jewelry and the jewelry box, so you set me up. What were you going to do to me out in the middle of nowhere?" she demanded, her blood running cold.

Another arrival in the hallway was much quieter,

but Macy recognized the handcuffed woman with another officer.

"And you had to be the one who posed as the buyer. You knew that the combination to Lisa's bank box was in the locket. You didn't want me to deliver the items in person because you didn't want me to know that the man from the grocery store was the victim's husband. And the killer. You people are greedy and sick! Shame on you! Lisa was a nice person!" Macy called out over her shoulder as Beadle propelled her down the hall, past the perpetrators.

CHAPTER SEVENTEEN

"Be glad you're a cat," Macy told the kitten who now followed her everywhere. "People can be awful sometimes."

When she'd returned home from the police station, Macy had thrown away her shoes and socks, and had soaked in the tub, scrubbing at her skin with a loofah until the thought of swampy water and thick mud finally left her. By the next day, she was feeling much more like herself, and met up with her shelter peeps for lunch.

Polly, Essence, and Sync were all waiting for her when she arrived at her favorite Mexican restaurant. Buzz wasn't one for social events, but he sent his regards and promised to keep the shelter running until the rest of them returned.

"Okay, girl, spill every drop of that tea," Essence demanded, munching on chips and salsa.

"Yeah, and don't leave any details out," Polly chimed in, raising her water glass.

"Unless you don't feel comfortable sharing," Sync added, patting her arm as she sat.

"Comfortable? They talked about her on the news. The least she can do is tell us more than they did," Essence challenged her mellow coworker.

"Only if she wants to," Sync said gently.

"Thanks, Sync. I'm pretty much fine now. I'm just glad it's all over."

"How did the cops even know where to find you?" Polly asked, before Sync could respond.

"So, the pizza guy who was the hitchhiker called them because he was so worried about the weird conversation that I had with him. He was also the one who positively identified Arthur, who had planned, as it turns out, to kill me and dump my body where he'd stashed the murder weapon," Macy recounted, with a shudder.

Sync's mouth dropped open, and he unconsciously reached out toward her, dropping his hand when Essence asked, "So, how do you know that he planned to kill you?"

"Regina Risinger spilled it all when Arthur tried

to throw her under the bus. She ended up being booked as an accessory to murder. I found that out when I took the rest of the victim's jewelry down to the police station for evidence. The desk sergeant called me a hero and gave me the lowdown."

"Accessory, jewelry … that's hilarious," Polly snickered.

"Excuse me, but no, none of this is hilarious," Sync blinked at her.

"Oh, lighten up, Ghandi, our girl Macy is still alive, and she has a cool story to tell at parties now," Essence gave Sync a look.

"Yeah, that's me, party animal," Macy smiled faintly.

"Speaking of animals … you have fur on your shirt." Sync made a brushing motion against his collar bone. "Did you get an emotional support dog?"

Macy laughed. "No, I rescued a stray kitten from a rainstorm. I'm just keeping her until I can find her a new home."

The other three exchanged knowing glances.

"Sure you are," Polly teased.

Macy pointed a chip at her. "You just wait and see."

"Mmhmm," Essence commented, as skeptical as the others.

"You gonna become a private investigator now that you cracked a murder case?" Polly asked.

"Please say no." Sync's eyes went wide.

"No worries, Sync. I've had my fill of law enforcement. I'm just going to walk dogs and sell cute vintage toys and jewelry that didn't come from a murder victim." Macy shook her head.

"And raise a stray kitten." Polly laughed.

"No way, no how. She's temporary, I swear."

"We'll see about that," Essence remarked.

"Cats are nice too, if you have the right aura," Sync added.

"Can't a girl just walk dogs?" Macy laughed and buried herself in the menu.

Food. She'd earned it.

**

If you enjoyed Show and Sell, check out Dog Eat Dog, book 2 in the Junkyard Dog Cozy Mystery series, next!

ALSO BY SUMMER PRESCOTT

Check out all the books in Summer Prescott's catalog!

Summer Prescott Book Catalog

AUTHOR'S NOTE

I'd love to hear your thoughts on my books, the storylines, and anything else that you'd like to comment on—reader feedback is very important to me. My contact information, along with some other helpful links, is listed on the next page. If you'd like to be on my list of "folks to contact" with updates, release and sales notifications, etc.… just shoot me an email and let me know. Thanks for reading!

Also…

… if you're looking for more great reads, Summer Prescott Books publishes several popular series by outstanding Cozy Mystery authors.

CONTACT SUMMER PRESCOTT BOOKS PUBLISHING

Twitter: @summerprescott1

Bookbub: https://www.bookbub.com/authors/summer-prescott

Blog and Book Catalog: http://summerprescottbooks.com

Email: summer.prescott.cozies@gmail.com

YouTube: https://www.youtube.com/channel/UCngKNUkDdWuQ5k7-Vkfrp6A

And…be sure to check out the Summer Prescott Cozy Mysteries fan page and Summer Prescott Books Publishing Page on Facebook – let's be friends!

To download a free book, and sign up for our fun and exciting newsletter, which will give you opportunities to win prizes and swag, enter contests, and be the first to know about New Releases, click here: http://summerprescottbooks.com

Made in United States
North Haven, CT
31 March 2024